Praise for

WISHYOUWAS

Shortlisted for the CrimeFest
Best Crime Novel for Children

'An instant classic'
Piers Torday, award-winning author of
The Last Wild

'A lovely and enchanting read. Letters, intrigue,
cute furry creatures – nine-year-old me would
have turned to this charming book over
and over again!'
Lesley Parr, author of *The Valley of Lost Secrets*

'A first-class festive adventure'
Daily Express

ALEXANDRA PAGE

ILLUSTRATED BY
Penny Neville-Lee

BLOOMSBURY
CHILDREN'S BOOKS
LONDON OXFORD NEW YORK NEW DELHI SYDNEY

BLOOMSBURY CHILDREN'S BOOKS
Bloomsbury Publishing Plc
50 Bedford Square, London WC1B 3DP, UK
29 Earlsfort Terrace, Dublin 2, Ireland

BLOOMSBURY, BLOOMSBURY CHILDREN'S BOOKS and the Diana logo are
trademarks of Bloomsbury Publishing Plc

First published in Great Britain in 2021 by Bloomsbury Publishing Plc
This edition published in Great Britain in 2022 by Bloomsbury Publishing Plc

A catalogue record for this book is available from the British Library

ISBN: HB: 978-1-5266-4121-2; PB: 978-1-5266-4122-9; eBook: 978-1-5266-4119-9

2 4 6 8 10 9 7 5 3 1

Typeset by RefineCatch Limited, Bungay, Suffolk
Printed and bound in Great Britain by CPI Group (UK) Ltd, Croydon CR0 4YY

To find out more about our authors and books visit www.bloomsbury.com
and sign up for our newsletters

With all my love to Andy, for sharing this journey

with me from the very first word

AP

For Mum and Dad

PNL

1
The Sorter

It was a rat.

At least, Penny thought it was.

A small shadow dropped out of the letterbox on to the doormat, then scuttled across the floor of the post office, trailing a thin, worm-like tail. Penny froze where she sat on the window sill, her skin prickling. Through a crack in the curtains, she followed its path along the edge of the darkened room. It darted behind a wastepaper basket.

Must be looking for food, Penny thought, hoping that once it found only old paper and envelopes in the bin it would leave. But a second later it re-emerged and scurried under the ledge where customers filled in forms. From there it moved in quick jerks, getting closer and closer to the long wooden serving counter. It crouched at the bottom, almost like a little customer itself, and for a moment Penny smiled. Then she jumped as the shadow leaped on top of the counter.

Penny heard something drip and glanced down with a groan: the fountain pen she was holding had spattered all over the letter she'd been writing to her mother. The date – *21st December 1952* – was now a blotchy, ink-stained mess.

By the time she looked back up, the rat had vanished and the post room was silent. Somehow, *not* knowing where it was made her goosebumps rise even more.

Penny left the pen on the sill and wiped her inky hands through her black hair. She slipped the letter inside her satchel, slid off the window sill and scanned the room.

It was too dark to see much. She lifted a curtain, but barely any light seeped through from the street lamps beyond the bay window. The great smog had blotted everything out – all the streets and houses and buses and people were lost somewhere in the thick haze of chimney smoke and fumes. Even the postbox outside the window was a shapeless red smudge.

Penny lowered the curtain and stiffened. A scratching sound was coming from behind the counter. Then she heard a *click*, like something being unlocked. But that didn't make any sense. There was nobody else in the room except her and the rat. What was it *doing*?

Swallowing her nerves, she tiptoed closer and ran her eyes over the spotless countertop, the polished brass weighing scales and soldier-like row of letter stampers. Nothing moved there. She peered at the sorting frame on the back wall, with its rows of cubbyholes for sorting letters. Beside it stood cabinets stacked with stationery for sale. She couldn't see any sign of the rat there either.

Then she caught the unmistakeable sound of a drawer sliding open. The hairs on her neck stood straight up.

I should tell Uncle Frank, she thought – and straight away changed her mind. He'd demand to know why she was in the post office out of hours, and that would mean losing her precious hiding place, from where she could catch the first glimpse of her mother. Penny's worries rushed up – *What if Mum flies her plane back to London too soon, then lands badly in the smog and … ?* She shook herself and squashed the thoughts back down. She had to be brave. Starting with the rat.

Penny lifted a hatch in the counter and ducked through to the other side, but it was too shadowy to see anything. She fumbled inside her satchel for her torch, clicked it on and shone the light along a row of drawers.

She startled as a sharp *crack!* echoed around the room, followed by a terrible, high-pitched squeal. Penny waved the torchlight. At the far end of the counter one of the drawers was ajar, the handle rattling madly on its hinges. She tensed, expecting the rat to wriggle out at any second. Instead the drawer began to shake and a muffled squeaking came from inside. Was it stuck?

Penny edged nearer. As the torchlight hit the gap, the drawer fell still. She reached for the handle, then stopped herself. If she freed it, the rat might leap out and bite her. She opened the stationery cabinet and chose a large, stiff brown envelope. Holding it in front of her as a shield, she reached out a finger and gave the handle a swift tug, then jumped back.

Nothing happened.

Penny craned forwards, but all she could see inside the drawer was an addressed envelope and a few loose paperclips. She took a tiny step closer.

There! Wedged in the back corner was a trembling brown lump, balled up like a pair of socks, not at all as terrifying as she'd expected. Penny lowered her envelope, feeling silly. Tea-coloured fur shone soft as velvet in the torchlight. And something silvery glinted beneath it.

'Oh!' Penny gasped. 'A trap!'

The small ball shifted, revealing a smear of blood

on the bottom of the drawer. The spring of a rat trap had snapped on to the middle of its slender tail, slicing the skin open.

'You poor thing!' Penny said. 'So *that's* why you couldn't get out.'

As she spoke, a small round ear popped up, followed by another. Then two huge, white, watery eyes peeped up at her, like miniature moons. They glistened in the torchlight. It didn't look much like a rat at all, close up.

Peering into Penny's eyes, the strange creature unfolded a paw. Four long, twig-like fingers reached towards her.

Penny felt her heart squeeze. She couldn't leave it like this.

Resting her torch on the counter, she pulled her coat sleeves over her hands. 'Please don't bite me!' she said. Inch by inch she reached in until she could grasp a corner of the trap. The creature balled itself tight as she levered up the metal spring, just enough for it to whip its tail out. Penny snatched her hands away.

There was a soft, sucking sound, and the creature

began to uncurl. Four pink paws emerged. Then a nose poked out, not sharp like a rat's, but stubby and soft, more like a kitten's, with a white streak down the middle and a small, upturned mouth beneath it. The little creature crouched on long, folded-up legs and sucked its tail, keeping its huge eyes locked on Penny's.

She noticed a paperclip dangling from a string around its neck. She reached in again to untangle it, but the creature popped its tail out of its mouth and scurried backwards.

'Don't kill me!' it squeaked.

Penny froze, her hand hovering in mid-air. 'W-what?' she stammered, blinking hard. She'd imagined it, she *must* have. After a moment, just to be sure, she said, 'Can ... can you say something else?'

The creature puffed its chest out as if trying to look bigger, but said nothing.

Penny reached towards it again.

'Keep back!' the creature warned, bunching its paws.

Penny's breath rushed out of her. She shut her

eyes and pinched her hand in case she'd fallen asleep on the window sill, but when she looked again the creature was still there, raising its tiny fists at her.

'I isn't afraid of you!' it said.

Penny realised how giant she must seem, even though she was small for ten. She knelt so that her face was on the same level as the creature's, and smiled. 'Don't be frightened, I won't hurt you, I promise!' she said. 'I think it's cruel to trap rats.'

The creature's fur darkened and its cheeks swelled as if it had swallowed two marbles. 'I is NOT a rat!' it burst out. 'I is a Sorter. Second Class,' it added, jutting out its tiny chin. Then its eyes widened and it slapped both paws over its mouth, dropping its injured tail.

Fresh blood welled from the Sorter's wound. 'I'll find you a bandage,' Penny said. 'Don't go away!' She rifled through the drawers until she came across a sheet of red tuppenny-ha'penny stamps with the new Queen's head on them. She tore one off. It was the perfect size.

The Sorter shrank into the corner as she reached into the drawer once more. It squirmed so much it was difficult to get hold of, but at last she managed to pinch the end of its tail between her fingers and wrap the stamp around the cut. When she let go, the Sorter grasped its tail and stared at it, stroking the curled-up face of Queen Elizabeth. After sniffing the stamp and whirling in a circle to see it at all angles, the Sorter turned to face Penny and, looking into her eyes, held out a spindly paw.

'I is Wishyouwas,' it squeaked.

Penny held out her finger and Wishyouwas's velvety paw curled around it, sending warm tingles up her arm. 'I'm Penny Black,' she said, grinning.

'Is you a he or a she?' asked Wishyouwas, tilting his head.

Penny snorted. 'A she,' she said. 'What about you?'

'I is a he,' Wishyouwas answered.

'I could see you weren't a rat,' Penny said.

Wishyouwas ruffled his fur. 'Humans always think we is. My pa was killed by poison.'

'I'm sorry,' Penny said. 'I lost my father too, in the war.'

Wishyouwas shuffled closer. 'Does you live here?' he asked.

Penny shook her head. 'I'm staying with my uncle as an emergency. He's the postmaster here. I live on the other side of London with my mum. She's an airmail pilot – you know, flying letters and parcels.'

Most people frowned or tutted whenever they heard that, as if it weren't the sort of job her mother should do. Uncle Frank didn't seem to approve either, because he wasn't happy when he had to collect Penny from the childminder three days ago. But Wishyouwas's eyes stretched wide and his cheeks lifted in a way that made her feel proud.

'She only does short trips,' Penny added. 'But this time she got stuck in France and can't fly back to London because of the smog. She telegrammed my uncle to ask him to look after me, but there was

11

no return address.' She remembered the unfinished letter in her satchel, which she'd add later to the growing pile of unsent letters in her room. A lump started to rise in her throat, so she asked instead, 'What about you? Where do you come from?'

Wishyouwas fiddled with his tail. He seemed about to answer when his ears pricked on high alert. A second later Penny caught a series of small thuds against the ceiling, followed by the creak of footsteps descending the stairs.

'Quick, Wishyouwas, hide!' she said and switched off the torch. She stumbled out from behind the counter, ran to the window and scrambled on to the sill, drawing her knees under her chin. She had only just folded the curtains around her when a door inside the post office swished open and the ceiling light snapped on. Penny watched in horror as the fountain pen she'd left on the sill rolled towards the edge and toppled off with a clatter.

She winced as the *tap, tap, tap* of a walking stick crossed the floor, coming straight for her.

2

Caught Red-Handed

'Come oot from there ... NOW!'

Penny's heart plummeted. The curtains were wrenched open and Uncle Frank stood over her, gripping his walking stick. The handle was shaped like the head of a Scottish terrier and Penny thought her uncle looked the same, with his blazing amber eyes and bristling ginger moustache. He stooped and picked up her fountain pen, arching his eyebrows as he waited for an explanation.

Penny tried not to glance across at the counter as she clambered off the window sill. She hoped

Wishyouwas had hidden better than she had. 'I was writing to Mum,' she said.

'It's gone ten o'clock, you should be asleep!'

'I know, but … I want to watch in case she comes back.'

Uncle Frank's moustache tilted downwards. 'She'll return when it's safe to do so,' he said. 'Until then, please respect ma rules and remain in the living quarters. If you want to write letters, there's a perfectly functional writing bureau upstairs.'

'But—'

'That's final!'

Tears stung Penny's eyes. He could at least let her help in the post office during opening hours. It would be better than sitting alone in her room, worrying. But she kept all the words she wanted to say sealed up. Uncle Frank would never understand. He didn't seem to care about Mum, or her. She was just an inconvenience.

Uncle Frank held the pen at arm's length. As Penny took it he peered down at her hands. On top of the ink, her fingers were now spotted with Wishyouwas's blood.

'Did you get a paper cut?' he asked, his eyebrows creasing.

'It's nothing,' Penny said, wiping her hands on the back of her coat.

'Aye, and nothing bleeds, does it?' Uncle Frank pulled a starched handkerchief from his jacket pocket, embroidered with a gold Royal Mail emblem. 'Use this,' he said. 'Come, the first-aid box is in the kitchen.'

He turned and hobbled towards the door that led to the living quarters. Penny trailed behind him, checking everywhere for Wishyouwas.

She bumped into her uncle's back as he stopped and swivelled his head towards the counter. 'What the devil ...' he muttered, spinning round on his stick.

'Wait!' Penny said, but Uncle Frank had already lifted the counter hatch and spotted the open drawer on the other side. Penny squeezed past him and they ended up in a tangled mess of limbs and stick as Penny tried to cover the drawer from sight while at the same time he reached around her to open it wider.

'Penelope!' he thundered. 'Oot of ma way!'

Penny glanced over her shoulder and slumped in relief. Wishyouwas wasn't inside. But the empty, bloodstained trap was.

Uncle Frank's mouth dropped open. 'Don't say that you set a rat *free*?'

'He was hurt,' Penny explained. 'The trap caught his tail. And then—'

'*He?*'

'He – it wasn't a rat,' she stammered. 'It could talk.' She instantly wished she hadn't said it.

Uncle Frank stared at her as if she were a talking creature too. 'Christmas is the busiest time of year!' he said, letting out a long breath through his nose. 'Everything is topsy-turvy because of the smog, and now I've lost the chance to catch a rat that's been stealing letters. The last thing I need is you pretending it's a – a pet!'

Penny frowned. 'What letters?'

Uncle Frank leaned on his stick and lifted his free hand to touch a metal tag on a chain around his neck. 'Every now and again,' he said, sounding tired, 'a letter arrives which can't be delivered. Sometimes there's a mistake on the address, or the envelope has got wet or damaged. It's ma duty to keep it safe in case the sender or recipient comes to collect it. But whenever I look, it's gone! It must be a wee rat. Maybe it likes the stamp glue, or shreds the letters for its nest, who knows? I never saw the like of it when I was a postmaster back in Glasgow. But they're the plague of London post offices. I've lost three letters this past month.' He sighed. 'I must've forgotten to lock the drawer again, though I was sure I had.'

Penny glanced at the drawer behind her. She remembered seeing a letter in there before, among the loose paperclips. Now it was missing. She scrunched her nose. Why would Wishyouwas go to so much trouble for a letter, when he'd ignored all the paper in the bin? It didn't make sense.

Uncle Frank was writing something down in a small black notebook. 'I'll have to order more traps,' he muttered.

'Don't do that!' Penny said.

Uncle Frank shut the notebook with a snap. 'Rats have no place in post offices,' he replied, pointing at the counter hatch. 'And neither do wee children!'

Penny trudged out of the door into the corridor and traipsed upstairs to her small bedroom. It was normally her uncle's study and just as neat and tidy as the post office. The writing bureau smelt of polish and even the books on the shelves were arranged from A to Z. But her mind was much too messy to sleep.

Her gaze fell on several volumes of *Encyclopaedia Britannica* on the top shelf. Clambering on to a chair, she shoved aside *The Dog Handler's Training Guide* and pulled out the heavy, red leather-bound books. She sat down and looked through every page on animals, but there was no mention of Sorters.

What she did find was a thumbnail-sized illustration of a small round-faced creature that looked a bit like Wishyouwas: '*Discovered more than a hundred years ago on a remote Pacific island, the tarsier is a small, shy and highly intelligent primate that hunts at night and can jump great distances.*

With eyes bigger than its brain, it can see in the dark and is exceedingly difficult to catch.'

Penny pulled her unfinished letter from her satchel and turned it over to the blank side. She copied the drawing in pencil, before rubbing out a white stripe along its nose and adding a stamp bandage on its tail to make it look more like Wishyouwas. *Why did he take that letter?* she wondered as she drew. Her tummy knotted at the thought of him coming back and being trapped again – or worse.

She chewed the end of her pencil. *Maybe* … if she could find another undeliverable letter and put it somewhere safe in the post office without her uncle knowing, she could hide and wait for Wishyouwas to return, then warn him to stop!

She slipped the drawing back in her satchel in case Uncle Frank saw it, and clambered into bed. As she burrowed under the covers, her fingers half frozen, she clutched on to the thought: *Tomorrow I'll find him again!*

3

Dead or Alive

Penny faced the empty sorting frame and rubbed her hands together. She'd never seen the post being sorted for delivery, but it couldn't be that difficult. All the cubbyholes were labelled in alphabetical order.

The icy morning air wrapped around her, making her shiver despite her coat and the warm pair of Mum's old trousers that she wore, nipped in and cut short to fit.

She glanced at the clock above the post office counter: 5 a.m. In an hour, the postman would arrive to do the sorting before he went on his rounds. When her uncle got up and found out *she'd* done the sorting instead, hopefully he'd think she was trying to be helpful and never guess she was searching for an undeliverable letter.

Penny untied the label from a bulging mail sack, dipped her hand inside and pulled out an envelope. It was addressed to *Dr Sandford*, so she slotted it into the S cubby of the sorting frame. The next letter was for *Mrs Aldridge*, so she put it in A. She bounced on her toes as she slotted letter after letter into the frame, enjoying being busy and useful for once. After half an hour she still hadn't come across a letter that looked undeliverable, but there were many more to go.

Penny's arms began to ache as she emptied the first sack. She reached for the next one, then heard an engine chug and brakes screech outside. She stopped and listened. It couldn't be the postman, because he came on foot. A surge of hope bubbled up inside her. *Mum?*

She ducked under the counter and flew to the

window, pulling the curtain aside. She pressed her nose against the glass, squinting beyond the postbox to the road, hoping she might see a taxicab, but the smog was too thick. Then she spotted a dim, hunched figure, making its way towards the post office …

Penny ran and unlatched the front door, her fingers fumbling in excitement as she unhooked the chain and threw it wide open –

She gasped and fell back. It wasn't her mother. Nor was it the postman.

The figure filled the doorway. It was a man wearing a long brown overcoat covered with pockets. In the dim light the front of his bald head looked like a giant snout. Penny opened her mouth to shout for Uncle Frank, but the words stuck in her throat as he reached up and peeled a gas mask off his face with a wet sucking sound, revealing small dark eyes, a long, sharp nose and yellow teeth spread in a grin.

'S-sorry,' Penny stuttered, stumbling backwards. 'The post office is closed.'

'Oh, I'm not one of your customers,' the man replied in a slow, slithering voice. 'You, in fact, are one of mine. My name is Stanley Scrawl. It's my job to catch rats for the Royal Mail.' He jerked his thumb downwards. 'And this is Ripper. He's the best ratter in London.'

A wiry greyhound with bony ridges along his flanks slunk through the door, as silent as a ghost. He sniffed the letterbox, then circled Penny, trailing a tatty rope lead.

'You're a rat catcher?' Penny said, a chill creeping down her spine.

Stanley Scrawl reached inside one of his many pockets and fished out a grubby telegram, which he held in front of her. Penny couldn't read the tiny print, but noticed with a shudder that his little fingernail was over an inch long and sharpened to a fine point.

'The postmaster here ordered my services.' The telegram flashed back into the rat catcher's pocket. Penny shrank aside as he thumped through the doorway, wearing heavy hobnailed boots. 'Where is he?' he asked, sniffing the air.

'Um – upstairs,' Penny said, edging away. 'I'll get him …'

'I didn't mean the postmaster,' Scrawl said. 'I meant the rat. Show me where it was hiding, then I'll be gone in the wink of an eye.'

Penny swallowed. 'I haven't seen any rats,' she said, truthfully. She flinched as Ripper nosed her coat pocket, where she'd put her uncle's handkerchief after wiping Wishyouwas's blood off her hands.

'We'll see about that,' Stanley Scrawl said. 'Ripper, hunt!'

The greyhound lowered his muzzle to the floor and trotted towards the counter.

'A-ha!' The rat catcher's nostrils flared. He levered the hatch upwards and Ripper darted through and scratched at the last drawer. Scrawl thumped over, wrenched it open and pulled out the bloodstained trap. Penny shuddered as he lifted it to his nose and took a deep sniff.

'You've got an infestation,' he said. 'How'd this one get away?'

Penny shrugged. 'I don't know,' she said.

'What did it look like?' he asked. 'Get a close look?'

Penny bit her lip as Scrawl squinted one eye, searching her face. She shook her head, determined not to give him any clue about Wishyouwas.

Stanley Scrawl stared at her for a long moment. 'It's a shame I missed this one. It'll have to be caught though. You can't let vermin run riot in a post office.' Like a magician, out of a deep pocket he pulled a long string of fresh rat traps. 'I've got other sorts of traps in the van,' he added.

'No!' Penny said. 'Please don't, it's cruel!'

Stanley Scrawl snorted. 'You're a soft touch, I see,' he said. 'But I've got to do my duty, miss. Perhaps I'd be better off speaking to the postmaster?' He moved out from behind the counter, towards the inside door.

'Wait!' Penny said, running in front of him to block his way. 'I – I can catch it.'

Stanley Scrawl's eyes narrowed at her. 'Dead or alive?' he asked.

'Alive,' Penny said. 'I know I can.'

Scrawl scratched a wart on his chin with his long fingernail. His eyes gleamed. Then he nodded.

'All right,' he said. 'Try it your way.' He dropped the traps back inside his pocket and Penny breathed out in relief.

'But I'll be back,' Scrawl added suddenly, leaning his face towards Penny until his nose was almost touching hers. 'If you don't catch it by tomorrow morning, I'll set the best trap I've got. I'm going to flush out every last one of them.'

He stood straight and whistled. 'Come, Ripper!' he ordered. He thumped to the front door and opened it with an icy blast. Wreaths of smog drifted inside. 'See you soon,' he said, with a greasy grin. He pulled the gas mask over his face and stepped outside, tugging Ripper's lead. The smog swallowed them.

Penny closed the door and leaned against it, her heart racing. When an urgent knocking came from the other side, she jerked in shock. She opened the door warily, but it was only the postman, Bert. 'I'm late,' he panted, pulling off his scarf. 'This stupid smog made me take the wrong turning. I'm late doing the sorting.'

'I've done it already,' Penny said.

'Really?' He smiled and checked his watch. 'Thanks a bundle! I've even got time for a cuppa!'

After he went through to the kitchen, Penny hurriedly finished sorting the letters. As she slotted the last one into the frame, her shoulders slumped.

Wishyouwas didn't stand a chance against the rat catcher. She still didn't have an undeliverable letter, and only had one day to find him.

4

Wishyouwas Returns

Penny traipsed into the kitchen, where the postman was brewing tea. She was soon warmed by billowing clouds of steam, and it made her feel better listening to Bert, who talked as if he couldn't pour his words out fast enough.

'... It's only thanks to the secret underground railway that anything's getting delivered at all,' he said, chomping into a slice of shortbread.

'What's the secret railway?' Penny asked, carefully spooning a tiny amount of sugar from the ration jar for her tea.

'Oh, it's brilliant!' Bert mumbled, scattering crumbs. 'I mean, it's not really a secret, but not many people know about it. It goes underground from Paddington to Whitechapel, carrying the mail. Imagine – hundreds of thousands of letters and parcels whizzing right beneath our feet, every day and night! Good thing we have it too, because the smog means the vans are taking forever to deliver the post.'

A sudden shout made their teacups rattle.

'Penelope Black!' Uncle Frank roared from inside the post office. 'WHAT HAVE YOU DONE?'

Penny jumped and the precious sugar tipped off her teaspoon on to the floor. As she bent down and tried to scoop up the crystals, the kitchen door flew open.

'Did you let her sort the post?' her uncle demanded, pointing at Bert.

The postman's cheeks turned bright red.

'It was my idea,' Penny admitted.

Uncle Frank let out more steam than the kettle.

'When we sort the post, we do it alphabetically – by *street name*,' he said. 'We'll have to re-sort it *all*.' He checked his watch, then glared at Penny. 'Because of this delay I'll need you to help in the post office today – and *only* today,' he warned, holding up a finger as Penny began to grin. 'You must do *exactly* as I say, and don't speak to the customers unless you are spoken to first. Is that clear?'

Penny nodded. Even though she was in trouble, she found herself smiling. Now she could keep watch for any undeliverable letters.

At opening time a long line of customers formed in front of the counter, muffled in scarves and heavy shawls as they carried in bags and baskets full of Christmas cards and parcels tied with string. Their gossip and chatter made the post office feel friendlier, despite Uncle Frank's scowl as he watched Penny like a hawk.

'What a year it's been,' muttered a cheerful-looking woman wearing a brightly coloured shawl, as she handed a parcel over the counter. 'First the King dies, rest his soul. Now this terrible smog.

Still, at least Christmas is around the corner. It's the only thing keeping everyone's spirits up!'

'I wish it would keep my spirits up,' mumbled an old gentleman behind her, his eyes watery. 'There's no chance of family visiting me this year. I'll be on my own!'

'Oh, Mr Andrews, you poor soul,' said the lady kindly. She turned back to Uncle Frank and her eyelashes fluttered. 'I think it's lovely that you've invited your niece to stay for Christmas,' she said. 'You're normally on your own too, aren't you?'

Uncle Frank's cheeks reddened and he made a sound like he'd swallowed a coin. 'It's – uh – ma pleasure to have her to stay,' he said.

Penny listened as she counted change and tore off stamps, weighed parcels and sold stationery. But at no point did her uncle or anyone mention an undeliverable letter. Her hope started to fade along with the gloomy grey light outside the window. Then snow began to fall, and the customers thinned to a trickle.

At five o'clock her uncle switched the sign on the door to CLOSED and hobbled back to the counter. 'You did well today,' he said gruffly. 'I'll be glad of some help again tomorrow … if you like?'

'Yes thanks,' Penny said, but her voice came out flat.

'Is anything wrong?' Uncle Frank said with a frown.

Penny shrugged. 'I tried to find something, but I couldn't.'

Uncle Frank drummed his fingers against the terrier handle of his stick. 'Well,' he said. 'When I've lost something, it's usually in the most obvious place. Talking of which, do you still have ma handkerchief?'

'Upstairs in my satchel,' Penny said. After Scrawl had been, she'd hidden it in there along with her torch and unfinished letter. *That's it!* A bolt of excitement ran through her. Of course! She didn't need to *find* an undeliverable letter – she already had one!

'Thanks, Uncle Frank!' she said. She caught his startled look as she ran out.

'I want ma handkerchief!' he called behind her.

In her room, Penny unlocked the writing bureau and pulled down the lid. From her satchel she pulled out the crumpled, ink-stained sheet of paper with her unfinished message to Mum on one side and her drawing on the other. She found an envelope in the bureau and folded the letter inside, licking it shut. She addressed it to *Captain Nora Black, France.* Then she licked her finger and smudged the address until it was unreadable.

The rattles and clanks of Uncle Frank cooking supper sounded from the kitchen. Penny tiptoed downstairs and through the hallway, eased open the post office inner door and sneaked behind the counter. She tried the drawer but found it locked, so instead slid her letter underneath the till, leaving a corner poking out. All she had to do now was wait and hope Wishyouwas would find it.

After bedtime she waited, wide awake, until she heard her uncle's tapping steps along the landing. As soon as he had closed his bedroom door she slipped out of bed wearing her satchel and stole downstairs. She plucked her coat from the kitchen coat stand and crept into the post office.

Her breath puffed out like smoke in the frosty air. Her letter was still there, under the till. She sneaked across to the window and tucked herself on to the sill, clutching her torch. The smog outside was thick as soup and snowflakes formed white ridges on the windowpanes.

The clock ticked and Penny's eyes began to droop. She rested her forehead against the icy glass to keep herself awake, fighting her sinking eyelids …

Something rattled.

Penny wobbled awake and almost fell to the floor. Her body was stiff with cold. What time was it? Pulling the curtain aside, she squinted at the clock – half past eleven! She'd slept for ages!

As her eyes adjusted to the dark, she saw something move on top of the counter.

Penny tumbled off the sill and staggered forwards, flashing her torch at the till.

Wishyouwas let out a terrified squeal. The Sorter had her letter clenched in both paws and cringed away from the light. Before Penny could say anything he leaped on to a shelf behind the counter.

'Wishyouwas, it's only me!' Penny breathed.

Wishyouwas's legs were like rubber bands. In a single powerful spring he landed on top of the ceiling light, making it swing wildly.

'Stop, Wishyouwas!' Penny pleaded.

Wishyouwas gave his tail a catlike flick, bounded off the ceiling lampshade and landed on the post office front door handle. Lowering himself to the letterbox, he pushed open the flap with one back paw and wriggled his bottom through, pulling Penny's letter after him.

Penny hurled herself forwards and grabbed a corner of the envelope an instant before it disappeared. She clung on with her fingertips as Wishyouwas struggled furiously on the other side of the flap.

'Give it to me!' he squeaked.

'It's not yours!' Penny gave a sharp tug. Wishyouwas popped back through the letterbox, dangling from the envelope by one paw.

'Please, Dear Penny, I has to take it!'

'Why?' she said. 'What are you stealing letters for?'

Wishyouwas dropped on to the doormat. He glared up at her and his fur darkened. 'I isn't stealing it. I never stole nothing!' he said, stamping one long-toed paw. 'I already told you, I is a Sorter. I is doing my duty as a Gatherer, Second Class!'

'But what does that *mean*?'

Wishyouwas pursed his mouth and looked away.

'Fine,' Penny said, fed up with being nice. She was only trying to help him. 'I'll keep the letter.' She lifted it above her head.

Wishyouwas threw himself flat at her feet. 'Dear Penny, *please* let me take the letter. I will get downgraded if I doesn't. I already got a warning because of the bandage you gived me!'

Penny peered down and noticed the red stamp was missing from his tail. A thick scab was in its place.

'I'm sorry,' she said, lowering her hand. 'But I got into trouble too for setting you free. You have to stop taking letters.'

'I *has* to take them. It is my duty,' Wishyouwas squeaked. His moonlike eyes pleaded up at her.

'Why do you want them?'

Wishyouwas shook his head vigorously.

'Please tell me. Then I can help.'

'But I isn't allowed, Dear Penny!'

'If you show me, then ... I'll let you keep this one,' Penny offered, holding her letter out.

Wishyouwas glanced at the door, then back at Penny's letter, wringing his paws.

'If I show you,' he said slowly, 'does you promise to keep it a secret?'

Penny nodded. 'I promise.'

Before she knew what was happening Wishyouwas jumped up, whisked the envelope from her fingers and scrambled out through the letterbox.

5

Into the Tunnels

Penny unlatched the door and poked her head out. 'Wishyouwas?' she called, as loudly as she dared. Her breath came out in nervous puffs. 'Where are you? Come back!'

She squinted through the freezing air, but Wishyouwas had vanished into the swirling smog. He'd tricked her!

Penny slumped against the door, her eyes stinging with cold and disappointment. Then, by the doorstep she spotted a long-toed paw-print in the snow. She crouched and shone the torch closer. A trail of prints! If she was quick, she could follow him.

She stepped outside and her heart beat faster. Uncle Frank had absolutely forbidden her from leaving the post office, but if she lost Wishyouwas now she might never see him again. She glanced over her shoulder – as long as she kept the post office in sight, nothing bad could happen.

Penny shut the door softly. Her footsteps crunched as she picked out the line of paw-prints in the torchlight. They ran beneath the post office window, then veered towards the snow-capped red postbox. The trail ended at its base. Frowning, Penny peeked into the letter slot.

She jumped as a moist nose touched hers and Wishyouwas's eyes gleamed in the dark. 'I was waiting for you, Dear Penny!'

'You were? I thought you'd run away! Why are you in here?' Penny asked, but Wishyouwas disappeared again. Lower down she heard a metallic clinking, followed by a scraping sound. Next moment the postbox door swung open.

She bent down and peered inside. An empty mail sack hung down from a hook at the top. Wishyouwas crouched in the narrow space beneath it, clutching her letter in one paw and his twisted paperclip necklace in the other. *He must have used it to pick the lock*, Penny realised.

'You has to get in the sack!' Wishyouwas urged.

'Why?' she asked, but then heard the faint *crunch, crunch* of footsteps.

With a jolt of panic Penny switched off her torch and stuffed it in her satchel, snatched the sack off its hook and scrambled into it, yanking it up to her chest. Then she squirmed into the postbox, jammed her knees under her chin and tugged the door shut, ready to pull the sack up over her head in case anyone looked in.

Crunch, crunch, crunch …

Penny strained her ears, hardly breathing as the footsteps came right up to the postbox. Through the letter slot she caught a glimpse of a colourful shawl before a white envelope tumbled on top of her head. She held on to it, stiff and scared, until with a rush of relief she heard the person's footsteps grow fainter. She pulled the sack down. 'I have to go back inside, Wishyouwas,' she said. 'Can you show me where the letters are now?'

'I *is* showing you,' his muffled squeak answered from near her feet. He wriggled and grunted, as if trying to pull something. Penny had a sudden nervous feeling.

'Wait!' she said. 'What are you—?'

The floor jerked and collapsed beneath her. She shrieked as her legs shot downwards and her insides squished upwards at the same time. She plunged into a black hole. Wind whooshed past her ears and whipped her plait behind her. She clutched the sack with all her strength as she slid faster and faster, swerving right, left, then right again, with nothing but darkness all around her. Her teeth rattled with the speed.

Then she felt a change. Little by little the pipe became less twisty and steep. She began to slow down. Snatching a breath, she heaved her head up and saw a speck of dim light ahead, growing larger. Then with a sickening lurch she shot into empty space and plummeted downwards …

Whumph!

Penny squelched into something soft and spongy. She rolled on to her back and lay still, groaning. Everything was spinning.

Her plait was given a sharp yank. 'You has to get up!' a voice squeaked in her ear.

'Wishyouwas?' Penny croaked. She rolled sideways and his eyes shone into hers like two coins. He pulled her plait again.

'Ouch, stop it!' Penny said, pushing herself up, still holding the envelope. She wriggled out of the sack, put the letter inside her satchel and pulled out her torch. She switched it on and let out a gasp. She'd landed on a mound of sacks at the bottom of a massive circular chamber. It towered above her, dotted all around with black holes, like the inside of an enormous, hollow tree. Cobwebs clung over the holes. It smelt ancient and forgotten.

'Where are we?' Penny wondered, her voice echoing up the chamber.

'We calls it the Arrivals Room. Lots of the postboxes in London has pipes going here,' Wishyouwas said.

Penny scrambled off the mound in case a heavy sack came thudding down on her.

'But people doesn't use them any more,' Wishyouwas added. 'Humans is always digging holes in the ground and forgetting.'

'How do we get back out again?' Penny asked. She swung the torch beam over several bricked archways that led off the chamber into low, narrow tunnels.

Wishyouwas bounded off the sacks and sniffed the air. 'I is taking you back later. We has to get to the burrow!'

'Where?' Penny said.

Wishyouwas scampered to the entrance of one of the tunnels. Penny edged up to it and shivered. Two rusting rails ran along the ground, disappearing into darkness.

'We has to go this way if you want to see the letters, Dear Penny,' Wishyouwas said.

Penny took a shaky breath. There wasn't much choice. Holding the torch in front of her, she shuffled into the tunnel, feeling it close in behind her.

'Slow down!' she called in panic as Wishyouwas scampered on all fours ahead of her, clutching her letter in his mouth.

Wishyouwas turned and ran back, then leaped

on to her shoulder and gripped her plait in his paw for balance.

Penny smiled as his warm fur brushed her cheek and his tail curled round her neck. She felt safer as they moved on.

The tunnel walls were ribbed with metal girders, like the inside of a giant snake. Every now and then Penny caught a musty whiff that made her nose wrinkle. Wishyouwas tugged her plait to move faster when this happened, his ears pricked high. They stayed quiet, only Penny's footsteps making any sound.

She was about to ask how much further they had to go, when they reached a junction where the rails along the ground joined up with another set. Penny's torchlight glimmered over a sign on the wall ahead of them:

← WESTBOUND – PADDINGTON

EASTBOUND – MOUNT PLEASANT →

'Which way?' she whispered.

Wishyouwas pointed east. Every few steps he swivelled on her shoulder and looked behind them. It was making Penny nervous. The musty smell wafted past them again and Wishyouwas stiffened, gripping his lock picker. A moment later Penny heard a faint scratching noise behind her. She spun round.

Something was creeping out of the darkness towards them.

6

The Front Gate

Wishyouwas jumped off Penny's shoulder and scampered towards the noise.

'Wait!' Penny called out, waving the torch to try and keep him in sight. She stumbled forwards a few paces and then stopped.

At the edge of the tunnel, a small, sleek shadow slid into view, creeping against the curved brick wall. A sharp, twitching nose, black eyes and an oily body slithered towards her. Her breath stopped with dread – she wasn't in the post office any more, where Uncle Frank was only a shout away.

Suddenly Wishyouwas pounced out of nowhere on to the rat's back. The rat gave a maddened screech and twisted, trying to sink its teeth into the smaller but much faster Sorter.

'Wishyouwas!' Penny cried, bursting forwards to save him. But he had already jumped clear and bounded back to her, before leaping on to her shoulder.

'Run, Dear Penny!' he urged, panting hard, his lock picker clutched in one paw.

As Penny turned she glimpsed another two rats emerge from the darkness. Each was twice the size of Wishyouwas. There was no understanding in their eyes – only hunger.

Fear made Penny's feet fly. She sprinted, stumbling between the rails, but the *scritch-scratch* of the rats' claws only seemed to grow louder behind them.

She shrieked as something brushed her ankle. At the same time the rails along the ground shuddered and a different sound like clanging pots and pans sounded behind them, getting louder.

'Get against the wall, Dear Penny!' Wishyouwas squeaked above the clamour.

She flattened herself against the tunnel with seconds to spare.

Two bright beams punctured the darkness. With a shock of air a red train exploded out of the tunnel and sped past them in a blur, its wheels spitting sparks. Penny screwed up her eyes and clutched Wishyouwas against her as it rocketed over the tracks, missing them by a whisker. Then it rounded a bend, leaving a deeper sense of darkness as it disappeared with a final, fiery flash.

Penny gasped for breath. She peeled herself off the wall and flashed the torch shakily both ways.

The rats had vanished.

'Dear Penny, is you all right?' Wishyouwas's fur stood out in tufts.

She nodded, although her heart was hopping. 'The train scared the rats away – but the driver must have seen us!'

'There isn't no driver,' Wishyouwas said. 'The post train works all by itself.'

'You mean this is the secret railway?' Penny said, remembering what Bert had told her.

Wishyouwas didn't answer. He jumped off her shoulder across the rails to the other side. 'This way, Dear Penny, we is nearly at the burrow!' he said.

Penny hurried behind him. Around the bend the tunnel forked two ways. Wishyouwas led Penny to the right, but a few paces further on they reached a dead end. Penny shone her torch over a huge heap of rubbish. Wooden crates and cable reels, trolleys with missing wheels, threadbare brooms, stacks of broken boxes and all sorts of abandoned and unwanted things were dumped in a haphazard heap right up to the tunnel roof. 'There's no way through!' she said, looking backwards in case the rats reappeared.

Wishyouwas hopped through the hole of a worn-out van tyre, then poked his head out again. He beckoned Penny with his paw.

'In there?' she said doubtfully. She squeezed through after him, feeling her clothes and satchel snag on sharp edges as she crawled through the heap. Just as she worried she was going to get stuck, she emerged in front of a strange metal wall. It had once been the side of a Royal Mail van, which had been cut into a rough circle and riveted to the wall. All that remained was flaking red paint, the gold crown emblem and a round petrol hatch at the bottom, beside a thin horizontal slot.

'This is the front gate,' Wishyouwas announced, then handed Penny the letter she'd written. 'You has to post this here.' He pointed to the thin aperture.

Penny knelt and pushed the letter through the slot. Almost at once the petrol hatch opened outwards, spilling a thin shaft of welcoming light. Penny was about to peer inside when a gruff voice barked, 'You're late!'

A squat shape stood silhouetted in the opening. 'Think it's our duty, do you, guardin' the front gate all night long, waiting for a clumsy, no-good Gath—'

The voice stopped abruptly, and a Sorter squeezed itself through the hatch. He gaped up at

Penny, whiskers quivering. He was six inches high and almost as wide, with bulging arms shaped like chicken drumsticks. Fixed to his chest fur with a paperclip was a rectangle of cardboard with HANDLEWITHCARE printed on it. In one paw he held a fountain pen with a glinting nib, like a miniature spear.

'Hello,' Penny said.

'Get back!' he bellowed, aiming his spear at her right knee.

'What's goin' on?' Another guard emerged from the hatch, wielding a knife-sharp letter opener. He looked almost identical to the first, except for a jagged scar that slashed his face from his round ears to his thrust-out chin. FRAGILE was printed on his badge. He sprang back as soon as he saw Penny and aimed his spear at her other knee. He turned to Wishyouwas. 'Who's *that*?' he demanded.

Wishyouwas puffed his chest, but his voice came out as a feeble squeak. 'She is Dear Penny,' he said. 'You has to let us in.'

Fragile's wonky nose wrinkled. '*You* don't tell *us*

what to do, Gatherer. It's our duty to protect the letters. Only *we* decide who and what comes in and out.'

'But she brung a letter!' Wishyouwas protested.

Handlewithcare shrugged at his twin. 'I haven't seen a letter – have you, Fragile?'

'Not that *I* know of,' Fragile replied.

'I can show you!' said Wishyouwas. He tried to dive between the guards but they crossed their weapons in an X, knocking him backwards.

Penny scrambled to her feet. 'Stop it!' she shouted, scooping Wishyouwas into her hands. 'There's a letter there and you know it!'

The guards held their ground as they glared up at her.

'The rules says you has to let in anyone with a letter,' Wishyouwas said, rubbing his head.

'But there isn't a letter,' said Fragile. 'So get packing!' Jabbing their spears in the air, the guards edged backwards towards the hatch.

Penny swallowed. 'You should go in,' she said to Wishyouwas. 'You'll be safe inside.'

He clutched her finger. 'I isn't leaving you behind,' he said.

A thought sprang into Penny's head. 'Wait!' she ordered, just as the guards were about to duck through the hatch. 'You said it's your duty to protect letters.'

'So?' said Fragile.

'So, you haven't protected *my* letter. It's missing and I'm not leaving it behind.'

The guards stopped. They glanced at each other,

then Fragile squinted at Penny. 'No letter has *ever* gone missin' on our watch,' he growled, but she noticed his long toes twitching.

'It has now,' she pointed out. 'Unless … it's behind the gate?'

Fragile's wonky jaw chewed on her words. Then he nodded at his twin and Handlewithcare disappeared through the hatch, reappearing a moment later with Penny's letter on the end of his spear.

'Found this,' he muttered sourly.

He lifted it towards her, but Penny shook her head. 'Anyone who brought a letter is allowed in,' she said.

Wishyouwas gazed up at Penny with his mouth open. She grinned back at him.

The guards' fur bristled. Scowling, they stood aside.

'Come with us,' Fragile ordered. His scar puckered. 'As for you,' he snarled, pointing at Wishyouwas, 'you're in a *parcel*-load of trouble.'

7

The Bureau

Hinges squealed and the front gate creaked open, flooding the tunnel with warmth and light. Penny stepped inside, blinking in the sudden brightness. Wishyouwas leaped on to her shoulder.

'Follow us,' Handlewithcare ordered, while Fragile heaved on a rope to close the gate. 'We're reporting you to Their Highnesses. They rule The Bureau.'

'I thought you called it the *burrow*,' Penny whispered to Wishyouwas.

He ruffled his fur. 'I is never saying it right.'

Penny smiled. 'It doesn't matter,' she murmured,

as the twin guards marched either side of them. Twinkling Christmas lights strung along the tunnel ceiling guided their path. Peeling posters with slogans like 'Post Early This Christmas!', 'Are You Pulling Your Weight?' and 'Pack Your Parcels Carefully!' papered the walls in bright colours. The air smelt like a library and she could hear a chattering noise, growing louder.

'This is where we take the letters, Dear Penny,' Wishyouwas squeaked as they rounded a bend, and she felt him puff up with pride.

Penny stared. A tangled web of ropes zigzagged across the tunnel, forming bridges between ancient-looking bookcases and shelving units, stepladders and dented filing cabinets, like phone wires between the buildings in London. Sorters scampered along the ropes in a busy hive of activity, while wicker baskets on wheels, large enough to hold a person, hurtled along the ground, veering from side to side as Sorters hauled them along on ropes. Everywhere Penny looked Sorters carried envelopes in their mouths, their round eyes fixed ahead of them.

'There are so many of you!' she said.

The nearest Sorters snapped their heads round in her direction. They blundered into each other and envelopes fluttered to the ground. Shouts erupted from the Sorters behind them.

'Move along there!'

'Stop blocking the line!'

'Rope hog!'

Then those Sorters spotted her too and the ropes swayed as they crashed and lost balance, clinging upside down by their paws. 'It's a human!' they squeaked.

Penny felt a sharp point jab her shoe. 'Move!' ordered Handlewithcare.

She ducked under the ropes, treading slowly to avoid scaring the Sorters too much. Even so, they leaped and scurried for cover as she passed them.

Every piece of furniture bustled with activity and the air rustled as envelopes were whisked from one pair of paws to another. Inside one cupboard she saw Sorters see-sawing on an ink blotter, flattening a crumpled letter. They toppled backwards when they spotted Penny.

Something rattled above her head and she saw long cardboard postal tubes connected together with tape. The tubes snaked along the roof before dropping towards the ground, where Sorters queued up clutching letters. One at a time they stood inside an opening above a whirring desk fan which shot them upwards at terrific speed. 'Like a lift!' Penny said.

'Pneumatic tube mail, actually,' answered one of the Sorters in the queue, before catching sight of Penny and falling over in a dead faint.

'Wishyouwas, what do you use the letters *for*?' Penny asked.

He opened his mouth to reply but Fragile barked, 'No more questions!'

Sorters scurried everywhere Penny looked. Hundreds of round eyes met hers as she stumbled along. A side tunnel branched off the main one, but the guards marched her past too quickly to glimpse what was down there. Then they came to an area of the main tunnel with two long rows of rectangular letterboxes, attached to wooden posts stuck in the ground. Some were red, some blue and some green. They faced each other like houses on stilts, each with its own number above the letter slot.

'Is this where you live?' Penny whispered to Wishyouwas.

He nodded and shuffled closer to her ear. 'Mine is One Hundred and Two. The green letterboxes is for Gatherers. Blue ones is for Solvers. One day if I is upgraded to a Deliverer, I get a *red* one.'

'Ah, I see,' she said. The red letterboxes were smart, with ROYAL MAIL stamped on them in gold, whereas the green letterboxes looked older and many were crooked. She spotted number 102 – one of the shabbiest, perched like a lopsided parrot on its post. A taped-on pencil stub replaced the number 1.

Round, whiskery faces peeped out of the letter slots, but vanished as soon as Penny smiled at them.

At the end of the two rows, a tall red postbox stood in the centre of the tunnel, like the one she had climbed inside. A pocket watch dangled on a long chain from the letter slot, ticking quietly with the hands at quarter past two. On the floor beside the postbox sat a set of rusted weighing scales. Instead of measurements, the dial showed the words 'Standard', 'Tracked', 'Priority' and 'Urgent'.

Everything in the Sorters' home had once been something broken or thrown away, Penny realised with a pang. Behind the postbox a curtain sewn together from frayed mail sacks covered the wall, with a magazine cutting of the Queen pinned to it.

The guards halted and Fragile yanked on the watch chain. Penny heard a faint *ting-a-ling-a-ling!* from inside the postbox and felt Wishyouwas's paw tighten around her plait.

Narrow eyes above a pinched face appeared at the letter slot, level with Penny's nose. She was about to introduce herself when the eyes slid to the ground and a voice demanded, 'What in parcel's name is the meaning of this interruption? Declare yourselves!'

'Stampduty, we found a human outside the front

gate with Wishyouwas,' Handlewithcare answered, bowing low. 'We've come to report it to Their Highnesses.'

'I see,' Stampduty replied. 'The "it" you have come to report is, I assume, your failure to do your duty and guard The Bureau?'

Fragile's scar scrunched into a knot. He raised his letter opener at Penny, even though she cast a huge shadow over them. 'No, Stampduty, the human. It brought a letter.'

'And has it been taken to the Solvers as per Rule Eighteen, Section Three, Clause Two (B) of the Law?' snapped Stampduty. '"*Every item gathered must be inspected for authenticity and processed as quickly as possible.*"'

The guards blinked.

'Well, no …'

'You see …'

'Enough!' A yellow HB pencil emerged from the letter slot, grasped in a pale, skinny paw. The pencil rapped against the front of the postbox, where a white rectangle displayed post collection times.

'You are all aware of the strict timetable. The next Audience with Their Highnesses is at four o'clock. I will not allow unscheduled deliveries to interrupt the normal operation of The Bureau.'

Handlewithcare stuck up a paw. 'But it's not a delivery, it's a *human*.'

'I can very well see that,' said Stampduty. 'Nevertheless it brought a letter and as such shall be treated in accordance with our rules. The Gatherer brought it, therefore the Gatherer is responsible for it.' Stampduty narrowed his eyes at Wishyouwas. 'Take it and the letter away and bring both back here in time for the Audience.' Then he peered down at the guards. 'As for you two, I suggest you return at once to your posts, in case any more deliveries arrive unannounced. After all, the cat is somewhat out of the bag now.' The pencil whipped back inside the postbox and Stampduty vanished.

Fragile shot a startled look at his twin. 'Did he say *cat*?'

'Uh, I think so,' said Handlewithcare. He flung Penny's letter to the ground and the twin guards shouldered their spears and raced back to resume their posts.

Wishyouwas hopped on to the ground and picked up the letter. 'Now I can show you what we does with the letters, Dear Penny,' he said, his eyes gleaming. 'First we has to go and find a Solver!'

8

The Law of the Letter

Wishyouwas led Penny back the way they'd come, before turning into the side tunnel. They passed an old refrigerator which emitted a sickly-sweet pong and the sounds of chewing. The fridge door was open and Sorters huddled on the shelves inside, nibbling green-speckled crusts of bread, mushy brown apple cores and vinegary-smelling chips with shreds of newspaper still stuck to them.

A little further on stood a tall cupboard, inside which a dozen or so Sorters lay in shoebox beds, several with limbs tied up with string. A harassed-looking Sorter wearing a napkin as an apron ripped small lengths of parcel tape off a dispenser and wrapped it around a torn ear, then moved on and bandaged another patient's bleeding forepaw.

Penny wondered how many Sorters had been hurt, or worse, in post offices like her uncle's. She began to creep past, not wanting to disturb them, but then by the wall opposite she spotted a wooden school desk with a tiny, pipsqueak voice coming from it, and couldn't resist stopping to see.

The desk lid rested open against the tunnel wall, displaying a handwritten postcard stuck on with drawing pins. A line of old stamps picturing different monarchs decorated the top of the lid. Inside the desk, a class of twenty finger-tall Sorters perched on cotton reels, facing a tall, elegant Sorter with splashes of grey mixed into her fur, and a blue silk handkerchief tied around her neck. She pointed a pigeon feather at the handwriting on the postcard as a little Sorter with a stuck-up quiff recited, '*The food on board is tem ... tem ...*'

'*Terrible*,' finished the teacher, rolling her r's in a soft voice. 'You must watch out for double r's, they can look similar to m's. An easy mistake to make. Very good, Yourstruly, you may sit down. Now, who can tell me who might have written this?'

A dozen tiny paws shot up. Penny hovered closer.

'A human on a ship!'

'Do not interrupt, Writesoon,' the teacher

scolded. 'Give the others a chance. And when was this postcard sent?'

No paws went up this time.

She flourished her feather at the top-right corner of the postcard. 'Pay attention to the date on the postmark. This particular postcard dates from nineteen – Oh!' She broke off and stared up at Penny, followed by forty button-like eyes. An instant later the tiny Sorters exploded out of the desk, shrieking and screaming and falling over each other like a box of firecrackers.

'Silence!' their teacher cried. 'Go to your places!' She grabbed at tails, paws and ears. 'Returntosender, stop that infernal noise. All of you back to your seats!'

'I'm sorry,' said Penny. 'I didn't mean to scare them.'

'Nonsense,' said the teacher. 'There is absolutely nothing to fear.'

Writesoon climbed to the top of the desk lid, which started to wobble. Penny lunged her hand out to stop it falling and the tiny Sorter squeaked in terror and toppled backwards, sliding down into the desk and landing on his bottom with a soft thud. The others squealed with delight and rushed to have a go. The pupils seemed to forget about Penny in this new game. They even used her outspread fingers as a ladder to climb up the lid.

'Well, at least that has occupied them!' said the teacher. She curtsied to Penny. 'I am Felicitations, Headteacher.'

Wishyouwas jumped up into the desk. 'This is the same school I gone to, Dear Penny,' he said proudly.

'*Went* to,' Felicitations corrected him. She shook her head at Penny. 'Wishyouwas's grammar is incurable, I am afraid.'

'I like it,' said Penny. 'It's sweet.'

'Unfortunately sweetness does not earn one a pass in one's Solvers' exams,' said Felicitations.

Wishyouwas lifted his chin. 'I doesn't want to be a Solver. I want to be a Deliverer.'

'What are those?' Penny asked.

'Has Wishyouwas not already told you?' said

Felicitations. 'Then allow me. You see, we are *all* Sorters, but there are three different ranks: Gatherers, Solvers and Deliverers. Wishyouwas is a Gatherer ...'

'Second Class,' interrupted Wishyouwas.

'Quite so,' said Felicitations. 'It is his duty to visit post offices on his route, looking for letters – as he was doing when you helped him escape from the rat trap.'

'You know about that?' asked Penny in surprise. Several of the little Sorters paused in their play and sat down to listen, staring up at Penny with awestruck eyes.

'Indeed, your act of kindness caused quite a sensation!' said Felicitations. 'A stamp is an object of great value.' She raised an eyebrow at Wishyouwas. 'One cannot walk around *wearing* a stamp, particularly one with the new Royal Postmistress's head on it!'

Penny frowned. 'The Royal Postmistress ... You mean the Queen?'

'That is how humans refer to her, yes. She must be honoured and respected, not worn on one's tail.'

'Dear Penny gived it to me,' Wishyouwas said with a sniff.

'*Gave* it,' said Felicitations with a sigh. 'Next there are the Solvers, who specialise in deciphering letters. Once they have worked out to whom and where a letter belongs, they pass it to a Deliverer to deliver it. Each rank also has different classes, from Third Class through to First Class. Only Their Highnesses may upgrade a Sorter to another rank or class. Earning this honour can take many years, even a lifetime.'

Wishyouwas lifted his chin. 'I is already learning the POD. Deliverers has to know it by heart.'

'Wishyouwas means the *Post Office Directory*,' explained Felicitations.

Penny's mind whirred. 'But why do you take letters at all?' she asked. 'My uncle thinks you're stealing them.'

Felicitations' eyes widened. 'Steal? Never! We only gather letters which humans have abandoned or forgotten. We call them "lost letters". It is our most sacred law.'

'The Law of the Letter!' piped up Yourstruly, climbing on to Penny's finger, and the other tiny Sorters started to chant:

'The Law of the Letter is written in ink!
Its rules we obey without stopping to think.
We gather and solve and deliver what's lost,
Without causing trouble or damage or cost.'

'Well done,' said Felicitations. She winked at Penny. 'The song helps them to remember.'

Penny's cheeks flushed as everything clicked together in her mind. It was so *unfair*. The Sorters saved lost letters, and in return people trapped and hunted them like rats. 'You should tell someone what you do,' she said. 'To protect yourselves.'

Felicitations shook her head gravely. 'Remaining hidden *is* how we protect ourselves, Dear Penny. Not all humans are as kind as you. Perhaps you will understand if I tell you a little of our history.'

'But we has to see the Solvers!' Wishyouwas protested.

'Then I shall keep this brief. It is a story passed down with each generation of Sorters.' With her paws, Felicitations drew a circle in the air. 'Our kind originally came from a small Pacific island covered with forests. We lived in the wild, until one day, many years ago, humans discovered our home. At first we were so trusting that they captured a great number of us.'

Penny felt her fists bunch together as Felicitations continued.

'They carried us aboard a ship, which also bore chests full of important letters bound for England. We sailed for weeks. All the while the crew attempted to tame us, so that they could sell us as expensive pets. We listened and learned their strange speech. After all, we did not know then that it is not usual for animals to speak as humans do. But then one stormy night, everything changed.'

The tiny Sorters squeaked in alarm and curled into balls. Even Wishyouwas stopped fidgeting.

'Mountain-high waves crashed, lightning struck the mast, and our ship splintered to pieces and sank into the depths. The captain and crew drowned, but the wooden chests full of letters floated to the surface. We managed to pick them open with our paws and drifted in them for days. Eventually we washed up on the shores of England. People discovered the chests and took them by mail coach to be presented to the King at Buckingham Palace. The letters had saved our lives and were all we had left, and so we followed them, to London.'

Felicitations lifted her chin. 'Life was hard for us, at first. We were prey to animals and humans who saw us as nothing more than food or pests. Until, escaping chase, one of us climbed inside a postbox and discovered a hidden pipe beneath it that led to these tunnels, where we made our home. Letters had saved our lives once more, and ever since then we have made it our purpose to save them, in return.' She clasped her paws together and smiled.

Penny jumped as a shrill ringing sounded and the tiny Sorters hopped into a neat line.

Felicitations hurried to the back of the desk and turned off an alarm clock. 'By parcels, three o'clock already! I must escort my pupils home before the Audience, Dear Penny.'

Penny felt a bump against her leg as a wicker trolley squealed to a halt beside the desk, pulled by two panting Sorters. The pupils hopped inside one by one, followed by Felicitations.

'Goodbye, Dear Penny!' she called, waving as the trolley took off. 'And good luck at the Audience. Whatever happens, remember you have friends here!'

9

Thiswayup

Penny paced behind Wishyouwas, chewing her lip as he guided her further along the tunnel. She had to find some way to protect him, but how could she if nobody knew who the Sorters were and what they did?

Wishyouwas stopped in front of her and she glanced up to see a familiar object against the tunnel wall: a large wooden sorting frame.

'Here is the Solvers, Dear Penny,' he said.

Penny peered into the cubbyholes. In each one sat a Sorter, with a letter, a postcard or an envelope pinned to the wall in front of them. Some held up old-fashioned monocles like magnifying glasses, squinting through the lenses at the handwriting. Others chewed pencil stubs, then darted forwards and scribbled tiny notes in the margin of a letter. The sorting frame was as quiet as a library and the Solvers were so absorbed by their work that they didn't notice Penny.

'What do we do now?' she whispered.

'We has to find a Solver who is available.' Wishyouwas pointed at the chalked labels beneath each cubbyhole. Most read '*Occupied*'. Then, in the bottom-most corner, Penny spied one that was blank.

'There!' she said, kneeling to see inside. Wishyouwas hopped forwards and knocked against the wood.

Curled up with his front paws crossed over his rumbling chest, and one back paw resting against the wall, slept a Sorter so old that his fur had wizened to white wisps and his face was a mushroom of wrinkles. A silver-rimmed monocle dangled around his neck.

Wishyouwas knocked again and the Solver turned over with a snore. Penny blinked in shock – he only had one back paw. The other finished in a stump where his knee-joint should have been. He slept on a messy bed of pencil sharpenings and a metal drawing compass lay beside him. A blueprint took up one wall, covered with diagrams of Sorters wearing what looked like different-shaped wings, scribbled all over with sums and equations. Old used stamps of King George and other monarchs from before Penny was born decorated the rest of the cubbyhole.

'Shall we try someone else?' she murmured.

Wishyouwas shook his head. 'We is lucky. Thiswayup is a First Class Solver.' He grabbed the compass and rapped it against the wall. 'Wake up, Thiswayup!'

The Solver woke with a snort. 'Eh? Who's that? Ah, Wishyouwas. And – oh my!' Thiswayup rubbed his misty eyes and focused on Penny's face through his monocle. He crawled to the edge of his compartment and, reaching out a paw, lightly prodded her knee. 'Bless my stamps, that's not a girl, is it? A human girl? I must still be dreaming. I was just having a marvellous dream about biscuits. I say, you don't happen to have a biscuit, do you?' he asked Penny. His nose twitched hopefully.

'No, sorry.' Penny giggled.

'I can't be dreaming then. Otherwise you would certainly have had a custard cream in your pocket.' Thiswayup sat up, held out a paw and shook her finger. 'You are Dear Penny, I presume? I've heard all about how you helped Wishyouwas escape the trap. It made me think of my old gathering days, before this –' He wiggled his half-leg. 'Still, once my flying invention is ready, I hope Sorters shall never again be at the mercy of dogs, or any predators, for that matter. The humans have airmail.' He tapped his blueprint. 'High time we caught up, don't you think?'

'Dear Penny's ma flies letters!' Wishyouwas said.

Thiswayup's mouth gaped. 'Your mother is an airmail pilot?'

Penny felt herself blush as she nodded. 'I want to be one too, when I'm older.'

Thiswayup clasped his paws together. 'A fellow aviator! Perhaps, if it is not too much trouble, you would care to give your thoughts on my invention?'

Without waiting for an answer, Thiswayup grasped the compass next to him and wriggled his leg stump into the pencil holder, turning the screw to tighten it. Grunting, he wobbled to his paws and, using the compass like a crutch, *tap-tapped* out of his cubbyhole and hobbled around the corner of the sorting frame. Penny followed him, until they reached a dented filing cabinet further along the tunnel. From somewhere among his folds of fur Thiswayup pulled out a small brass key and turned it in the lock.

'Would you be kind enough to open the bottom drawer, Dear Penny?' he asked, rubbing his paws.

Penny pulled it open. Inside was a heap of strange triangular objects. She picked one up and turned it over in her hands. 'It's a coat hanger!' she exclaimed. Brown parcel paper covered the triangle part, and the hook had been bent into a loop beneath it.

'I call it a *hang-glider*,' Thiswayup explained. 'Wishyouwas, would you care to demonstrate?'

Wishyouwas dropped Penny's letter to the ground and leaped on top of the cabinet. Penny handed him the glider and he grasped the loop in both paws. A concentrated frown scrunched his face.

With a flick of his tail, Wishyouwas leaped off the edge and the hanger took flight. Penny caught her breath as it rose promisingly, up and up, before the tip hit the ceiling and then plunged like an arrow towards the ground. She threw herself forwards and grabbed it an instant before it crashed.

Wishyouwas dropped safely to the floor, looking thrilled.

Thiswayup shook his head. 'There's still a problem somewhere. Thank you, Dear Penny. I have got through a great deal of hangers … and volunteers,' he added with a sigh.

Penny tipped the glider in her hands. 'Here,' she said, pointing to the front. 'The weight is too far forward. If you add extra loops for his back paws so Wishyouwas can lie flat, the pivot point will move backwards and it should fly more evenly.'

Thiswayup's eyes widened as he took the glider from her. 'By parcels, you might be right!' He turned it over with his paws. 'A little string here and there …' He looked up at her and his face folded inwards. 'I must apologise, Dear Penny, it seems among all the excitement I have forgotten my manners. How may I be of service to *you*?'

'We brung this,' Wishyouwas said, hopping forwards with Penny's letter.

'Let me see …' Thiswayup took the letter, then rubbed his monocle on his fur and held it above the envelope. Peering closely, he felt all around the edge with his long fingers. 'Standard letter, definitely not a HIVE,' he muttered.

'What's a HIVE?' Penny murmured to Wishyouwas.

'High Value Envelope,' he said. 'They is letters or parcels with valuables inside. We has to be extra careful with those.'

Thiswayup held Penny's letter up to the light. 'One hundred micrograms Norwegian parchment, almost certainly supplied from a post office,' he said, then lowered it and sniffed the ink. 'Only written a day or so ago, by a young hand. Hmm …' He squinted at the smudged-out address. 'Hard to tell for sure, but I should almost say someone purposefully damaged the address …' He stopped and lifted one eye at Penny. 'This is not a lost letter, is it?' he said in a low voice.

'Yes it is!' Wishyouwas cried, his fur darkening. 'I finded it in the post office, didn't I, Dear Penny?'

Penny swallowed a lump in her throat. She'd only wanted to use it to find Wishyouwas, but now hiding the pretend lost letter seemed like a mean trick. 'I – I couldn't find a real one,' she admitted, 'so I wrote one myself.'

Wishyouwas jumped as if he'd touched an electric wire. 'But I already has a warning!' he squeaked, clutching his tail. 'And we has to take the letter to the Audience!'

'But it doesn't matter, does it?' Penny said, looking to Thiswayup for reassurance. 'I'll tell them it's my letter and that I said Wishyouwas could take it.'

'Bless my stamps, no!' Thiswayup said. 'Our Law is very strict, I am afraid. A Gatherer must never take a letter that isn't lost. Even by mistake.' He scratched his head. 'This *is* a fine pot of glue to be in.'

Penny watched Wishyouwas pick at the scab on his tail. The last thing she'd wanted was to get him into trouble.

'I know you meant well, Dear Penny,' Thiswayup said. 'But convincing Their Highnesses of that is quite another thing. Some years ago, a postman pretended letters were lost when they were not, all for his own gain. It caused a parcel-load of trouble. We must *not* let them think you have done the same.' Thiswayup tapped his monocle. 'But perhaps … yes!' He beckoned them closer. 'We will reverse the process!' he said under his breath. 'Strictly against the rules, of course, but for you, Dear Penny, I shall make an exception.' He licked his paw and ran it across the name and address on the envelope. 'We need a special solution,' he muttered. 'Follow me.'

He hobbled over to the sorting frame and crawled to the back of his compartment. Bits of wire, string and pencil stubs flew over his shoulder as he rummaged.

'Ah! Here we are – my very own secret recipe.' Thiswayup brought out an ink bottle and removed the cork stopper with his mouth. He dribbled a few drops of vinegary-smelling liquid on to Penny's envelope and the smudged words began to fade until they were completely invisible.

Thiswayup squinted at it, then nodded and passed the letter to Penny. 'Wave it about a bit to dry,' he whispered. 'Of course, it's only a quick fix to make it look like an unsolvable. Any Solver worth his stamps would guess it had been tampered with, but it should pass muster with Their Highnesses. Fortunately their eyesight is not what it once was.' He winked.

Penny marvelled at the blank envelope. 'Thank you!' she whispered back.

Wishyouwas jumped forwards to give Thiswayup a hug.

'You'll crush my bones if you're not careful!' The old Sorter waved him away, but his eyes gleamed. 'I *do* like to use my inventions,' he said. 'Every year my application to join the Novel Ideas Branch of Sorters is rejected. If you ask me, they wouldn't know a novel idea if it gave them a paper cut. That's why I keep my best ideas under wraps. Wouldn't want NIBS getting all the glory, eh?'

'Ouch!' Penny jumped as two needle-sharp points pricked her foot.

'We've been looking for you!' growled Handlewithcare, scowling up at her.

'Time for the Audience,' added Fragile. 'And don't forget the letter.'

10

The Audience

Hundreds of Sorters crowded between the rows of letterboxes and formed a semicircle around Their Highnesses' postbox. They edged away from Penny, muttering to each other as the guards escorted her to the front.

Penny took off her satchel and knelt. Wishyouwas crouched close beside her.

In front of the postbox a pile of red Post Office Directories created a makeshift platform. On top of these sat an open wooden box with two empty inkwells and a label inside the lid that read: *Royal*

Inks. Penny was about to ask Wishyouwas what it was for when the hands on the pocket watch dangling from the letterbox reached four o'clock, and a deep hush fell.

The postbox door creaked open an inch, and a pale, thin Sorter with narrowed eyes and a sharp protruding nose slid out. Penny recognised Stampduty, who had been mean to the guards. He clasped his yellow pencil in one paw and a small pocket notebook in the other, which he propped open beside him on the platform.

In his high, nasal voice he announced, 'All rise for Their Highnesses Dearsir and Dearmadam, Supreme Rulers of the Sorters of The Bureau, Keepers of the Law of the Letter, Loyal to the Royal Postmistress. All rise!'

The Sorters shuffled to their paws. A few moved further away from Penny as she clambered to her feet.

The postbox opened wider and Penny caught a glimpse of the inside, wallpapered with ancient-looking letters. Two grey, flabby Sorters waddled out of it holding swan-feather quills, and nestled their bulky behinds inside the empty inkwells. Red wax seals embossed with crowns adorned their necks, like medals. They squinted down their noses at the gathered Sorters.

Stampduty waved his pencil for the Sorters to sit, and Penny knelt. 'There are three items on today's agenda,' he read from the notebook. 'The first order of business is from the Deliverers.'

To Penny's right the crowd parted and a muscly Sorter marched to the front. He wore the dial of a wristwatch around his neck and a handkerchief draped over his shoulders like a cape. One of his ears was bandaged in parcel tape. Penny thought she recognised him from the hospital cupboard. Despite his injury the Deliverer held his head high, with a furrowed, determined gaze.

'Your Highnesses,' he called out in a solemn voice, bowing low. 'My honoured title is Posthaste, Deliverer, First Class. It is my duty to inform you that in recent days, many rats have appeared in the train tunnels. Their swarms are growing in number, and they are coming closer.'

'All Sorters are to travel in pairs outside of The Bureau, until further notice,' Dearsir continued.

'Meanwhile,' added Dearmadam, 'our Threat Level will be increased and the rat situation tracked closely.'

Stampduty scribbled a note, then nodded to two Sorters who were standing beside the weighing scales Penny had seen earlier. They heaved an extra weight on top and the arrow on the dial swung from 'Standard' in green ink to 'Tracked' in yellow.

Posthaste bowed stiffly and marched back into the crowd.

'The next order of business is from the Gatherers!' called Stampduty.

Pushed to the front by a flurry of paws, a much smaller Sorter with inch-long eyelashes and a blue hair bow above one ear stumbled before the platform. She bobbed a curtsy, trembling from ears to tail.

'Name and rank?' Stampduty demanded.

The Sorter sunk her chin into her chest. Her mouth moved but no sound came out.

'Speak up!'

'W-Withlove, Your Highnesses,' she stammered. 'G-G-Gatherer, Second Class.'

'State your order of business, Gatherer.'

Withlove clutched her lock picker, staring around her with huge, frozen eyes. Their Highnesses bristled with impatience. Then Wishyouwas hopped forwards and touched Withlove's paw. She took a sudden deep breath and said, 'I have to r-report that my r-route is bl-blocked.'

'Blocked by what, exactly?' demanded Dearmadam.

Withlove lowered her eyes and spoke so quietly Penny could hardly hear her. 'A c-cage has been f-fixed to the p-post office letterbox,' she said.

Dearmadam frowned down her pointed nose. 'Very well, another route will be assigned to you until further notice,' she said.

Withlove gave Wishyouwas a shy smile and then retreated into the crowd.

'The last order of business is the human girl,' announced Stampduty.

'Her name is Dear Penny!' Wishyouwas squeaked.

Penny glanced at him gratefully as she stood. Paws shuffled and hundreds of eyes stared up at her. She swallowed.

'Girl,' Dearsir said. 'Tell us who you are and exactly what you are doing here.'

Even though she towered above them, Penny's knees started to shake. Their Highnesses peered at her, waiting. She had to get this right, for Wishyouwas's sake. She took a deep breath. 'My name is Penny Black. I came to find the lost letters,' she started. 'My uncle's a postmaster and he thinks rats are stealing them, so—'

'How did you find your way here?' Dearmadam interrupted.

Penny frowned. She hadn't had time to explain. 'I caught Wishyouwas,' she said. 'I wouldn't let him take the letter unless he showed me where he was taking it.'

'Bring forth the letter,' demanded Dearsir.

Penny's stomach knotted as she reached down and placed the envelope in his chubby paw.

Tap, tap, tap, tap.

Thiswayup hobbled out from among the Sorters until he stood between her and Wishyouwas, leaning on his crutch. 'I have already inspected that letter myself,' he panted. 'It is an unsolvable.'

'I should like to verify it,' Dearsir said. 'Fetch my glasses, Stampduty.'

Stampduty went inside the postbox and returned with a pair of cracked steel-rimmed spectacles, which he held above the envelope.

Not a sound disturbed the silence. *Please*, Penny thought, *don't open it!* Her drawing of Wishyouwas would prove it was hers. Her neck felt hot as Dearsir squinted through one lens at the invisible address. Then he handed the envelope to Dearmadam, who felt all around it as Thiswayup had done. Penny looked down at Wishyouwas, who was picking the scab on his tail so much it had started to bleed.

Dearsir and Dearmadam consulted, before raising their heads.

'This is indeed an unsolvable,' Dearsir announced. 'As a Gatherer, Wishyouwas was duty-bound to gather it. The girl has admitted she forced Wishyouwas to bring her here as well, therefore he is not to blame for her intrusion.'

Penny sagged in relief. Thiswayup turned and gave her and Wishyouwas a sly wink.

'However!' Dearmadam cried, making all the spectators jump. 'A Gatherer's first rule is "never be caught". Wishyouwas was trapped once already and received a warning. Now, he has been caught *twice*.'

'But it wasn't his fault,' Penny blurted. 'It was my mistake, not his! If I'd known—'

'Silence!' ordered Stampduty.

Dearmadam continued. 'In light of his clumsiness, Wishyouwas is clearly unsuitable for gathering lost letters. For his own safety's sake and that of all the Sorters, he is hereby downgraded to Third Class with immediate effect. His new duty is to gather food from the dustbins. Withlove shall take over his old route.'

'No!' Penny cried. 'You can't!'

But Stampduty had already hopped off the platform and removed Wishyouwas's lock picker, leaving him with a ring of ruffled fur where it used to be.

'You too are warned, girl,' Dearsir croaked. 'You see what damage is done when humans interfere with our world. Go home and never return.'

'The Audience is concluded!' Stampduty announced.

'Wait!' Penny shouted. '*Please!*' But the Sorters were already scattering back to their duties. Even Thiswayup hobbled away, shaking his head. Dearsir and Dearmadam waddled back inside their postbox, followed by Stampduty, and the door clanged shut. Only Wishyouwas didn't move. He stood still, staring at the postbox. His paws hung limply at his sides.

Penny fell to her knees. 'Wishyouwas, I'm so sorry! I didn't know this would happen. I should never have written the letter!'

His eyes were like lumps of ice. Without looking at her, Wishyouwas turned and ran away.

11

A Narrow Escape

Fragile and Handlewithcare marched Penny to the front gate. She stumbled along, her eyes so blurred with tears that she could barely see. The guards hauled on a length of rope attached to the old van door handle. The gate swung outwards, chilling her with a rush of cold air.

'Turn east until you reach the train platform,' instructed Handlewithcare. 'There'll be humans there. You can find your own way out, after that.'

Penny's hand trembled as she opened her satchel and pulled out her torch.

'One moment!' called a voice. Behind them, Thiswayup hurried forwards on his crutch, grasping an envelope. 'Dear Penny!' He waved it in the air. 'I have the unsolvable you gathered with Wishyouwas. Any letters we cannot solve are always returned to where we gathered them from. Perhaps you would be so kind as to take this?' He stopped, panting, and held it up.

Penny nodded and knelt to take it, but Fragile knocked her hand aside. 'Only Deliverers take letters out,' he growled, aiming his fountain pen at Thiswayup.

The old Solver drew himself up and balanced on his good leg. 'Don't point that twiddly stick at *me*, you impertinent ink blot,' he snapped. 'I have had far more practice wielding *this*.' He brandished his compass in the air, the point glinting. 'As for what is allowed in or out, consider yourselves lucky that Their Highnesses overlooked *your* roles in this –' he glanced at Penny – 'unfortunate situation.'

Fragile and Handlewithcare scowled at him, but then backed away.

Thiswayup pushed the letter inside Penny's satchel. 'Remember, Dear Penny,' he murmured, 'nothing is ever lost that cannot be solved.' He winked at her, then turned and tottered away.

Penny watched him go, taking one last look back at The Bureau. She wished she could undo everything she'd done, but it was hopeless. With a heavy sigh, she turned and stepped through the gate, which immediately slammed shut behind her. Pushing her satchel ahead of her she scrambled through the rubbish heap, her hair and clothes snagging on sharp corners, until she emerged on the other side. Before her the tunnel stretched on into blackness.

She shivered. Her shoulder felt empty without Wishyouwas perched there.

As she stepped forwards something squeaked behind her and she spun round, tingling with shock. But it was only an old trolley wheel spinning. She must have nudged it as she crawled through the heap. Beside it she noticed an old broom handle and wriggled it out. Gripping it tightly, she began to walk along the tunnel. Her breath sounded frighteningly loud in the darkness.

At the junction she paused and looked left and right, straining her eyes and ears. A cold breeze whistled past her and the sound of dripping echoed in the dark. Watery panic began to rise up inside her. *What if I get lost, or a train comes, or the rats … ?*

Suddenly she sensed something climbing up the broom handle.

Penny shrieked and let go, but whatever it was had jumped on to her arm. As the broom clattered to the ground, two moonlike eyes loomed in the torchlight.

Penny gasped. 'Wishyouwas?'

'Shh!' He raised a long finger to his mouth. 'I doesn't want nobody to know I is coming with you! I hided in your bag when Thiswayup gived you the letter.'

'But – I th-thought …' Penny stuttered, hardly able to believe it. 'I thought you didn't want to be my friend any more?'

Wishyouwas lifted his chin. 'Friends doesn't break promises.'

'But if Their Highnesses find out you came with me you'll be in even bigger trouble!'

'So is you, if you get lost,' he replied.

Penny hugged him against her cheek. 'Thank you! I'll make it up to you, I promise!'

'You doesn't need to, Dear Penny. It isn't your fault I is so clumsy.' Wishyouwas clambered on to her shoulder and curled his tail around her neck. Penny smiled.

'Are we going back to the Arrivals Room?' she asked.

Wishyouwas shook his head. 'We goes out the other end.' He pointed to the right. 'It isn't far.'

Penny began walking. Her spine prickled whenever she heard a sound and she noticed Wishyouwas reaching for his lock picker, which was no longer there. She'd forgotten to pick up the broom handle too. She sped up, her nerves crawling like ants under her skin.

They rounded a bend and a thin crescent of light appeared up ahead, along with the sounds of people. Penny's heart began to race with a new fear:

what would happen if someone caught her trespassing? She put away her torch and kept close to the tunnel wall as an underground station came into view. It was like the London Tube, only about half the size. A sign on the curved station wall read MOUNT PLEASANT – POST OFFICE RAILWAY HEADQUARTERS, and a clock hung down from the ceiling showing the time as a quarter past five. Parked beside the platform was one of the red mail trains and a line of open-topped carriages, looking small and friendly in the light. Penny

crouched in the shadows beneath the platform ledge, using it as cover. She peeped over the top, beside Wishyouwas.

A blur of legs and work boots pounded the platform a few feet away. Dozens of men and women in brown overalls unloaded the train carriages, their bodies hunched under heavy mail sacks. They hauled them off the train and tossed them inside large wicker trolleys, calling to each other in loud voices.

Above the bustle, Penny heard a clatter. More sacks tumbled out of a silver chute that protruded

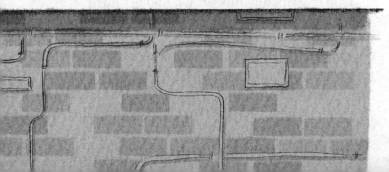

from the middle of the platform ceiling, landing on a conveyor belt that trundled them along and dropped them in a growing heap.

'Last sack off!' someone shouted.

A man poked his head out of a door marked *Control Office*, and barked, 'Load 'er up!'

The workers now pushed the trolleys aside, grabbed sacks from the end of the conveyor belt and started refilling the carriages.

'It's hopeless!' Penny whispered. 'I'll never get out without them seeing me.'

Wishyouwas's ears twitched and his head swivelled, following the movements of the workers. 'I know how we is getting out!' he said. 'Those trolleys is taken outside.' He pointed at a trolley nearby, loaded with sacks from the train.

'I still can't reach it,' Penny said.

Wishyouwas crouched low and wriggled his bottom. 'I is seeing you there,' he said.

'Don't!' gasped Penny. 'You could get hurt!'

But Wishyouwas sprang off her shoulder on to the platform. Her breath caught in horror as he scurried among the thundering boots. She lost sight of him, then further down the platform a man's high shriek split the air.

'Argh! A rat! It's on me! Get it off!'

The workers stopped and stared down the platform, turning away from Penny.

This was her chance! She scrambled on to the platform and crawled to the trolley while the workers dropped their sacks and ran towards the trouble.

'Stay still, Gary!'

'It's gone up my overalls! Help!'

Penny rolled herself inside the trolley, curled on to her side and heaved a sack on top of her. She burrowed herself beneath it as much as she could, panting in the musty darkness as the chaos continued:

'Calm *down*, Gary!'

'Wait, it's there – by the bin!'

'It's jumped on to the clock!'

'Where's it gone now?'

'Crikey, it's quick! I had no idea rats could leap like that!'

Come on, Wishyouwas! Penny cried in her head. All she could see was a tiny patch of the platform ceiling above the side of the trolley. *Where is he?*

Out of nowhere a furry brown ball flew across her vision and landed near her head. Wishyouwas scrambled beneath the sack and crouched beside her, his fur quivering. Penny could hear the workers still hunting around the platform, oblivious that the 'rat' had made its escape.

'They might have killed you!' she breathed. 'Next time I'll let them see me instead.'

Wishyouwas shook his head, his eyes gleaming.

'Get those trolleys out of here in case the rat gets inside one!' the man from the control office ordered, his voice muffled through the sack. 'I'm calling the Postmaster General.'

The trolley jolted forwards and someone wheeled them along the platform. Penny lay absolutely still. She felt Wishyouwas shrink down and his paw curled round her finger, as together they prepared to face whatever awaited them at the other end.

12

The Return

The trolley bumped and jerked. Penny struggled not to squirm as the heavy mail sack squashed her.

Over the trolley's edge she glimpsed more of Mount Pleasant. The worker wheeled them along a winding corridor. Then they entered a cavernous room, where the air smelt oily and clamoured with the hammering and whirring of tools. Fiery sparks crackled, reflecting in Wishyouwas's eyes, as they passed mechanics welding dismantled engine parts. The trolley halted.

'Orders are to take these sacks out straight away,' said the worker.

'Load them in the lift, mate,' said someone else. 'That'll take them up to the car park. The posties'll collect them from there.'

The trolley rumbled inside a sort of large metal box and a concertina gate rattled shut. Penny's stomach lurched as the floor began to rise. She'd never ridden inside a lift before. Wishyouwas didn't seem to have either, because his eyes widened and he wriggled nearer the edge of the trolley to see out. After a few seconds the lift shuddered to a stop, the gate opened and they were pushed outside into the cold night air.

The footsteps of the worker faded and disappeared.

'We is outside, Dear Penny!' Wishyouwas squeaked. 'There isn't nobody here. I can take you back now.'

Penny opened her mouth to argue that he had already helped her far enough, when Wishyouwas scurried back under the sack and raised a finger to his mouth, his fur on end.

Penny heard a low whine on the other side of the trolley, followed by shuffling footsteps. The hairs on her neck rose as a shadow fell over the trolley.

'What's this you've smelt then, Ripper?'

Penny wanted to tell Wishyouwas to run – to get away *now*! But the words died in her throat as the sack hiding them lifted up …

'You there! Stop!' shouted a commanding voice. The sack dropped back down.

'Postmaster General, sir! It's only me, Stanley Scrawl, your humble rat catcher.'

Penny could see Scrawl's long brown overcoat and the back of his round, bald head, which he ducked in a bow as a uniformed man marched up to him holding a lantern. His face was cold and stern.

'It is a good thing you are here, Mr Scrawl. The eastbound platform have alerted me to *another* rat infestation.'

'An infestation, sir?' Scrawl replied. 'I can't understand it. Night and day I've been laying my traps, doing my duty. If one or two have got away—'

'One or two hundred, you mean!' snapped the Postmaster General. 'They are becoming a plague!'

'It's the smog, sir. It's driving the rats underground,' Scrawl said. 'Perhaps, if I might be bold and suggest an idea ... shut the railway tonight, then I can get down in the tunnels and catch them.'

Penny stopped breathing. If the Postmaster General agreed, Scrawl might find the Sorters! She reached for Wishyouwas's paw and he clutched her finger.

'Tonight?' said the Postmaster General. 'Close the underground railway before Christmas Eve?'

'Yes, sir. I can't squeeze in them tunnels, what with the trains whizzing by every two minutes. Give me a couple of hours and—'

'It's the busiest night of the year!' the Postmaster General interrupted. 'The trains are already overflowing with extra post because of the smog. You must be mad!'

Stanley Scrawl sniffed. 'Forgive me, sir, but it's

the only way if you want the rats caught. After all, you wouldn't want any more alarms …'

But the Postmaster General's voice was as sharp as a pen. 'Either find another way to do your job, or collect your wages and go. I have already given you a second chance.' He glared at Scrawl, then swung round and marched away.

'Oh, I'll find another way all right, *sir*,' Stanley Scrawl muttered. 'Come, Ripper, we've got work to do.' His footsteps shuffled away.

Penny's heart galloped. 'Let's go now, in case he comes back!' she whispered.

Wishyouwas poked his head out, then crooked his paw to signal the all-clear. Penny scrambled out of the trolley and dropped to the ground in a crouch. The smog wreathed around her. Ahead, all she could see were the faint orbs of street lamps and vague, reddish shapes.

Wishyouwas beckoned her to follow him. Keeping low, she darted forwards and the dim red shapes revealed themselves as Royal Mail motor-cycles and vans.

They had almost made it to the end of the car park when a dog's shrill yapping broke the quiet and Penny stumbled. *Scrawl's dog!*

'Wishyouwas, go!' she said.

He leaped on to her shoulder instead. 'I isn't leaving you, Dear Penny.'

'You have to!' she said. 'I'll distract them.'

Wishyouwas shook his head.

'Get it, Ripper!' Scrawl shouted not far behind them.

'Please!' Penny begged, kneeling to put Wishyouwas back on the ground. 'I'll be all right, but it'll kill you!' Wishyouwas hesitated, then he jumped forwards and squeezed her finger. His eyes glimmered for an instant before he scurried underneath the closest van, out of sight.

Penny stood up and ran a few feet away, then waved her arms.

'Here!' she cried. 'It's only me, Penny, from the post office!'

The greyhound shot out of the smog like a grey bullet, trailing its lead. It swerved past Penny and scrabbled beneath the van where Wishyouwas had hidden.

'No!' Penny cried.

Stanley Scrawl appeared beside her. 'Ripper!' he yelled, grabbing the dog's lead and giving it a sharp yank. A low whine sounded in Ripper's throat as he skulked back to his master.

Scrawl stepped closer to Penny. 'What are *you* doing *here*?' he said, squinting at her.

Penny made herself look as frightened and timid as she could, which wasn't difficult. 'I – I got lost,' she stammered. 'I thought I could find a letter here.'

'What letter?'

'From my mother – but … there wasn't one.'

Scrawl's eyes darted around them. 'Where's your uncle? Isn't he meant to be looking after you?'

Penny opened her mouth, then shut it again.

'Don't tell me you came here by yourself, this early in the morning?' he asked, leaning closer still.

'I …' she said, trying to think of an excuse that

wouldn't risk him finding out about Wishyouwas or the Sorters, but her mind felt like a blank sheet of paper.

Stanley Scrawl straightened suddenly and grinned. He fished inside one of his many pockets and produced a van key. 'I'll drive you back,' he offered, jingling it.

'Oh, I wouldn't want to trouble you,' Penny said. 'I'm sure you're very busy ...' But Scrawl was already walking away.

'No trouble,' he said, glancing over his shoulder. 'Unless you want to ask the Postmaster General to telegram your uncle to come and collect you instead?'

Penny bit her lip. The further away Stanley Scrawl and his dog were, the safer Wishyouwas would be.

Scrawl crossed the car park and stopped beside a vehicle parked in the most shadowy corner, furthest from the street lamps. Even in the gloom, Penny could see it was the filthiest, most dented Royal Mail van she had ever come across.

'Hop in,' Scrawl said, opening the passenger door with a rusty squeak. He jerked his thumb at Ripper, who jumped inside and curled up on the floor. Penny clambered in, then Scrawl slammed the door and walked round to the driver's side. As he switched on the engine, black fumes belched out of the exhaust. By the time they'd exited the car park, swerving to avoid lamp posts and vehicles, Penny thought she was going to be sick.

Stanley Scrawl's van was truly disgusting. Foam bulged out of tears and splits in the upholstery and the floor was thick with crumbs in various stages of mould.

Penny heard something rattle and noticed a little white stick on a piece of string, dangling from the rear-view mirror. She leaned closer. It looked almost skeletal …

'Don't touch anything!' Scrawl snapped, making her flinch back. Then he eyed her sideways and smiled. 'I wouldn't want you spoiling my van. You look like you've been dragged through the tunnels backwards!'

Penny tensed and all too quickly checked herself in the mirror. Black smuts smeared her forehead and her hair was a nest of tangles from scrambling through the rubbish heap. She felt her cheeks redden and Scrawl's eyes narrowed.

'Have you caught that creature yet?' he asked.

Penny gripped her satchel. 'Um … not yet,' she said. 'But I'm sure I will!' she added, hoping Scrawl had forgotten his promise to come back and set his best traps.

'I don't blame you. It's taken me years to find a way to catch them,' said Scrawl. 'You can't outsmart them. You can't outnumber them. You'd have to be as fast as a *train* to outrun them.' He wrenched the wheel to avoid hitting a dustbin which loomed out of the smog, then glanced sideways again. 'I wish I knew their secret, don't you?'

Penny clamped her mouth shut. Her insides jumped about as the van bumped along the road. Scrawl gripped the steering wheel tighter and tighter. Then he slammed his boot on the brake pedal and the van screeched to a halt. Penny shied

away as he turned towards her. His yellow teeth flashed in a grin. 'Almost missed it! Here you are, back safe and sound.'

Through the grimy windscreen Penny saw the dim silhouette of the post office. The lights were still off.

'Thank you,' she said, clambering out of the van in relief.

'One minute, miss!' Stanley Scrawl heaved himself out of the van, shuffled round to the back and opened the door. Inside, Penny glimpsed long nets on poles, sacks and tottering piles of empty cages. Scrawl reached inside.

'I let you try catching it your way,' he said. 'Now we'll try mine.'

He pulled out a wrapped parcel the size of a shoebox. Producing a pen from one of his pockets, he scribbled something in large letters across the top, then held the box out to her.

'What's that?' Penny asked, without touching it.

'I invented it myself!' he said, tapping the top with his long fingernail. '*Scrawl's Handmade Unpickable Trap*. Soon there'll be one of these in every post office in the country – even the world!' He thrust it into her arms. 'Then every last one of those sneaky, conniving creatures will be gone, for good. Give that to your uncle. He can have this one for free.'

Penny forced herself to smile, but inside she grimaced as she read her uncle's name on the box. She had no intention whatsoever of letting the horrible thing come into the post office. Then a thought struck her. Why was the trap 'unpickable'? Rats couldn't unpick locks.

She looked up with a gasp, but Scrawl was no longer there. The van coughed fumes into her face and veered up the street, vanishing into the smog. Penny's hands shook, and it wasn't from the biting cold.

What if it wasn't rats that Scrawl wanted to catch at all?

13

Missing

Penny winced as the paperclip she was twisting pricked her thumb. Since dumping Scrawl's trap in the nearest dustbin and sneaking back into the post office, she'd been too worried to rest. Instead she huddled in her room, making a new lock picker for Wishyouwas. She planned to leave it in the post office one night with a genuine lost letter, then Withlove would find it when she came gathering and give it to him. Still, it wasn't much. Not nearly enough to undo all the harm she'd done.

She twisted too hard and the paperclip snapped.

Penny sighed and picked up another, stifling a huge yawn. Her thoughts kept returning to Scrawl, making her even more clumsy than usual.

If Scrawl was doing such a bad job at catching rats on the railway, why was he so interested in catching one at the post office? *Unless he knows about the Sorters*, she thought, her tummy squirming. But then how could he, if he wasn't able to get into the tunnels because of the trains?

She felt as if she were carrying a sackful of questions, and there was nobody she could ask. Not even Wishyouwas.

Finally she twisted the paperclip into the shape she wanted, like a tiny corkscrew with a small loop at one end. She threaded a length of string through it and tied a knot. *Finished.*

Footsteps creaked on the landing. Penny slipped the lock picker into a pocket of her satchel and switched off the torch. She listened as her uncle tapped his way past, down the stairs and into the post office. She fidgeted, trying to remember if she'd locked the post office door or not. But no angry shouts echoed upwards, and so she made her way down to the kitchen, blowing on her icy fingers. She turned on the stove, poured water into the kettle and popped two eggs inside it, then made toast.

Uncle Frank was a long time coming in for breakfast. *He's helping Bert sort the post*, she thought, as clattering and thumping sounded along the corridor. The kettle was whistling by the time he hobbled in, his face beaded with sweat.

'Morning, Uncle Frank,' Penny said, trying to sound normal. She reached a wooden spoon inside the kettle.

'Good grief – what *are* you doing?' he said.

'Soft-boiled eggs,' Penny replied, scooping one out. 'It saves time.'

Uncle Frank's bushy eyebrows jumped. 'Aye … I suppose it does,' he said. 'Just like your mother. She always found unusual ways to solve problems, when we were bairns.' He blinked and glanced at his watch. 'And time saving is exactly what we need today. It's the last chance to post in time for Christmas. I've already lost half an hour fitting that cage.'

Penny's egg wobbled on the spoon. 'Cage?' she croaked.

'Aye. The bin man spotted it and brought it in,' Uncle Frank said. 'I telegrammed Headquarters asking for the rat catcher. He must have dropped off the trap and gone, then someone put it in the bin.' He sounded pleased, pulling a letter opener from his pocket to butter a slice of toast. 'Clever contraption. It fits over the letterbox. That way anything that drops through gets caught. It prevents any wee rats getting in that way, at least.'

Penny's egg fell and splattered on the floor. 'You have to take it off!' she said.

Uncle Frank scowled at the mess. 'I don't have time for this, Penelope,' he snapped.

'Please,' she begged. 'You don't understand!'

'It's necessary.'

'No it's not!'

'Aye, it is!' Uncle Frank glared at her. Then his shoulders slumped. 'I don't like harming animals either,' he said, touching the small metal disc that

hung around his neck. His arm fell. 'But I … care about *you* more.'

Penny felt her cheeks redden. 'Oh,' she said. Maybe he *would* understand. She wished she could tell him about the Sorters, about what they really did. But she'd made a promise.

'And don't dare try and tell me,' Uncle Frank continued, pointing the letter opener at her, 'that rats are friendly. You were lucky not to lose a finger!'

'Will you please take off the trap?' she asked again.

Uncle Frank sighed. 'If it makes you happy, I will,' he said. 'But later. There'll be a queue longer than ma patience by the time we open.'

He was right. The moment Uncle Frank switched round the sign on the post office door, customers poured in. Penny could just glimpse Scrawl's trap behind all the coats and bags, a horrible-looking mesh of thin wire nailed over the letterbox. She worried about it as she helped, which caused her to make more than one mistake.

By lunchtime she'd counted out the wrong change twice and leaned on an ink pad, staining her elbow bright blue. Her uncle's moustache twitched more and more, until she dropped a whole pile of first class letters into the second class mail sack.

He aimed the end of his stick at the counter hatch. 'I'll manage on ma own from here, thank you, Penelope,' he said.

'But—'

'No buts! Go and rest, you look exhausted.'

Penny trailed out of the post office and walked upstairs in a daze. She slumped on to her bed and her eyes closed.

The next thing she knew she was falling down a giant black hole. She screamed into the darkness for help, and then remembered Wishyouwas. *I'm not lost, he'll find me!* she thought. Bright eyes glinted ahead of her and she reached towards them in relief. Only it wasn't Wishyouwas, but an oily shadow with sharp, gnashing teeth …

Penny jolted awake, sweat trickling down her back. She recognised the familiar shapes of the writing bureau and book shelves in her tiny, dark room and felt calmer. But then she remembered the letterbox trap and sprang out of bed – how long had she been asleep?

No sounds came up from the post office below. She shivered as she hurried downstairs, unable to shake the creeping feeling that something was wrong. The glass door that led into the post office was dark. She went into the kitchen, but that room was also quiet and empty.

On the table lay a folded piece of paper with her name on the front. She opened it and began to read:

6.00 p.m.
Penelope,
I received an emergency summons to Royal Mail Headquarters to help sort the Christmas post. There is dinner in the stove if you are hungry. I will be back later this evening.

I am sorry

Penny stopped reading as she heard a faint squeaking outside the kitchen back door, like someone walking in wet shoes. Was Uncle Frank back already? But then she listened closer – there was no sound of a stick. She lay down the letter, her heart thudding, and tiptoed to the back door. She peered through the glass, but the outside was so dark and blurred by smog that she couldn't see anything.

She leaped back as the door handle pulled downwards, then flipped up again, followed by a muffled thump and a squeak. Penny gasped. *Could it be ... but why come this way?* She turned the key and yanked the door open.

Glass smashed near her feet. Empty milk bottles rolled off the doorstep, bowled over by a furry brown ball. It uncurled and sat up in the snow, rubbing its head.

'Wishyouwas!' Penny said happily. Then her smile fell.

Wishyouwas's breath came out in faint squeaks. Ice frosted his fur. 'Thank parcels I finded you, Dear Penny!' he chattered. 'Something terrible has happened.'

'What is it?' Penny asked. She scooped him up and carried him inside.

'I camed here with Withlove,' Wishyouwas said, shivering in her hands. 'We left the burrow extra early to check you was safe. I waited for Withlove in the postbox when she went in, but she never comed back out.'

A cold, sick dread washed over Penny. 'The trap!' she said.

Wishyouwas nodded, scattering drips on to the floor. 'I looked in the letterbox and sawed a cage, Dear Penny, but Withlove wasn't there! I tried to find another way in.'

Penny glanced down at her uncle's letter on the table. Her stomach tightened as she read the final words:

I am sorry to tell you that I found a rat in the trap after closing time. The rat catcher has already been to take the rat away. I couldn't risk you getting hurt again.

Yours, F.

'Stanley Scrawl's got Withlove!' Penny gasped, leaping to her feet. She checked the kitchen clock: a quarter past six. 'He can't have been gone long – we have to find him and get Withlove back!'

14

Scribe's End

Penny dashed to grab her coat and satchel from the coat stand. But as she pulled them on, a hollow, hopeless feeling took hold of her. How *could* they find Scrawl?

Wishyouwas wasn't on the kitchen table when she turned round. Penny followed his trail of drips and found him inside the post office, perched on a shelf and tugging on a thick red-covered book. She helped him lift it down and laid it on the counter: *The Post Office Directory*.

'The POD!' she said, opening it in the middle.

Wishyouwas rifled through the pages. 'I hasn't learned *all* the addresses yet,' he said, stopping at the section beginning with S. He ran his paw down a long alphabetical list, then pointed at an entry in the book: *Scrawl, Stanley – Scribe's End, North London.*

'Yes!' Penny said. 'Can you find the way?'

Wishyouwas leaped on to her shoulder and nodded. 'It isn't far, Dear Penny.'

'Let's go!'

Penny rushed past the dim silhouettes of shops and houses, slipping and skidding on the snowy pavement. Her torch beam bounced off the smog, as if it were hitting a brick wall, but Wishyouwas squeaked directions in her ear.

The streets were almost deserted. The few times another person came past, Penny stopped in a doorway, in case they thought she was lost and tried to stop her. Her hands were numb when they eventually reached a narrow road, which was more of an alley, bordered by high brick walls. A lopsided postbox stood on the corner.

'We is here, Dear Penny!' whispered Wishyouwas.

A street sign on the wall gleamed in the torch-light: SCRIBE'S END. Penny's heart quickened as she began to creep down the road.

'I can't see any houses, can you?' she said, squinting to try and find a doorway. Wishyouwas shook his head. *Maybe it's a false address*, Penny thought.

But before they reached the end of the alley, a van loomed out of the smog and Penny caught a flash of dirty red paintwork. 'Scrawl's van!' she hissed, instinctively retreating.

Wishyouwas jumped down. He swivelled his head in both directions, nodded at Penny and scampered closer. Penny edged up to the dark windows. She peered through the grubby glass, but there was nobody inside. Creeping round to the back of the van, she saw the alley hit a dead end. 'Is this where Scrawl *lives*?' she wondered.

'Watch out, Dear Penny!' Wishyouwas squeaked. Penny froze just in time – her foot was hovering above a wide, dark hole in the ground. A metal manhole cover lay beside it. She stumbled back, gagging. A sickening, sewery stench seeped from the hole.

'Dear Penny, I heared something in the van!' Wishyouwas said. He jumped on to the back door handle, trying to yank it open.

'Wait, it might be him!' Penny said, but then she heard it too – a faint squeak for help.

She swung the door open and a thin, desperate voice called from inside, 'D-Dear Penny! W-Wishyouwas! Is that you?'

Wishyouwas darted inside. Penny clambered after him, shoving aside nets and cages. She looked up and a bolt of fear made her gasp – a figure loomed over them. But after a blink, she realised it was only a blue postman's uniform with a gold Royal Mail emblem on the breast pocket, like the one Bert wore at the post office. It hung from a coat hanger at the very back of the van. Beneath it lay a heap of squashed sacks, covered with a smelly blanket. And on the bed sat a small cage, even more vicious-looking than the one fitted over the post office letterbox. The top was fastened with a huge padlock and the wire bars were so close together, even the smallest of creatures could not have escaped. Two round eyes glistened from within and a thin, trembling finger reached through a tiny gap.

'Withlove!' Penny cried. 'Are you hurt?'

'N-no, but I couldn't p-pick the l-lock,' the small Gatherer squeaked.

'I'll carry the cage!' Penny said, but when she picked it up something clanked and pulled her back. Her heart plummeted as she saw a thick chain was bolted from the cage to the van.

Something thumped from the street behind them.

All three of them stiffened and stared out of the van. Fear surged up Penny's spine as she saw a dark shadow rise out of the hole in the ground.

'Stay down there, Ripper!' ordered a voice. With his back to them, Stanley Scrawl wriggled out of the hole and heaved a sack after him, which he dumped on the ground. It might have been a trick of the smog, but Penny thought the sack moved. Without looking round, Scrawl lowered himself down again and disappeared.

'He'll c-c-come back!' Withlove squeaked. 'D-Dear Penny, he is t-taking rats out of the sewers!'

Penny looked at the sack, which was definitely wriggling. *But why would Scrawl … ?* She shook herself. There wasn't time to think. She pulled on the cage, bracing her feet against the floor, and heaved, but the chain held firm.

'I can't do it!' she panted. 'We have to break the lock!'

'I t-tried,' wailed Withlove. She pushed two thin pieces of her lock picker through the cage. It had snapped in half, too short to be of any more use.

'Wait – I have another one!' Penny said. She rummaged in her satchel and pulled out her home-made lock picker. Wishyouwas sprang on to the lock and began twisting and rotating it with furious concentration.

'I'll try to find something we can break it with,' said Penny, searching the van. She lifted rags, knocked aside bottles and pushed over old card-board boxes, seeking any sort of tool. There was nothing. Then she remembered the coat hanger.

Climbing on to the dirty sacks, she reached up and unhooked the uniform, and as she did so her blood turned to ice.

Behind it, taped to the van wall, was a hand-drawn map. A thick black line snaked across the page, with names scrawled above it, including *Paddington* and *Whitechapel*. 'It's a map of the post office railway!' she said. The torchlight lit up big red X's scratched over all the stations except one: *Mount Pleasant* – which had a ring drawn around it. That was where the Sorters lived.

'D-Dear Penny!' Withlove said, peering through the cage. 'He t-told me that he has been p-planning this for years!'

'Planning what?'

'I d-don't know!'

Penny shook the uniform off the hanger and jumped down, her mind a whirlwind of fear and confusion. Wishyouwas hopped aside while she jammed the hook of the coat hanger into the lock. Together they wrenched it round but the hook twisted and snapped off.

'B-behind you!' Withlove squeaked.

Penny glanced over her shoulder. Scrawl's bald head emerged once more from the hole, puffing and cursing.

'Go!' Withlove urged.

'Not without you!'

'You have to t-tell Their Highnesses!' the Gatherer insisted.

Wishyouwas hopped on to Penny's shoulder.

'Withlove is right, Dear Penny. There isn't no choice.'

Scrawl was out of the hole and reaching back into it. Penny took one last look at the little Gatherer in the cage and stifled a sob. Then she squirmed out of the van, trying not to trip over the nets, and jumped out as Scrawl hoisted another sack out of the ground.

He spun round and saw them.

'Come here!' he snarled, lunging for Penny but missing by a whisker. She hurtled headlong down Scribe's End, tearing through the smog.

Wishyouwas tugged her plait. 'The postbox, Dear Penny!'

She almost collided with it. Wishyouwas leaped straight inside the letter slot, the lock picker still in his grasp. Penny checked behind her – she could see Scrawl's hunched shadow growing larger, hear his thumping feet and heavy breathing.

The postbox door swung open. Penny crammed herself inside and pulled the door shut. 'Lock it, Wishyouwas!' she said.

'The lock is broked!' he squeaked. 'The door was already open.'

Above Penny's head, two dark, glinting eyes appeared at the letter slot. Penny shrank down, while Wishyouwas scrabbled at her feet, searching for the mechanism …

'I might be too big to follow you,' sneered Scrawl, pointing his finger with the long sharp nail at her, 'but don't think I can't get you. The best way to catch a rat … is with another rat.' He yanked the postbox door open, just as the floor beneath Penny dropped with a jolt.

Penny plunged into the blackness of the pipe. Without a sack her knees and elbows bumped and grazed painfully against the sides. She curled up tight, squeezing her eyes shut, until she flew out of the hole at the other end, on to the heap of sacks at the bottom of the Arrivals Room. This time she clambered straight off. Wishyouwas waited for her beside the tunnel entrance.

Something *plopped* behind her.

Penny spun round. Small objects dropped

through the air on to the heap and beetled down the sacks. In the torchlight she saw the flicker of long tails and heard high-pitched screeching. Fear made her freeze, at the same time as an answer wrote itself in her mind: *That's why there are so many rats – Scrawl is using the postbox to send them down into the tunnels!*

Wishyouwas hopped in front of her, brandishing the lock picker, his fur sticking up like needles.

'Go, Dear Penny!' he squeaked.

The thought of him fighting the rats alone sprang Penny into action. She scooped him off the ground as the rats poured down, scattering in all directions. She backed towards the tunnel entrance, kicking away any that came too close, then turned and fled. Her satchel bumped against her side as she pelted between the iron rails.

They reached the junction and turned east. Still Penny kept running, her breath coming in ragged shreds. She didn't dare check behind them or pause for a moment. They took the right fork and at last the rubbish heap flashed in the torchlight.

Penny scrambled through the heap, then hammered against the front gate. 'Let us in!' she shouted.

Wishyouwas rapped the lock picker against the petrol hatch until it opened, and the spear-tips and ruffled heads of Handlewithcare and Fragile jutted out.

'*You* again!' They both scowled. The door swung shut but Penny shot her foot out, wedging it open.

'Stop!' she said. 'It's an emergency!'

'We're not falling for another of your tricks,' said Fragile, shoving her shoe backwards. He glared up at her.

'Yeah. We ain't stupid,' said Handlewithcare, beside his twin. 'We've got strict orders to keep all humans out!'

Penny's mind raced. 'But you *have* to let Wishyouwas in,' she said. 'Rats are coming!' The guards narrowed their eyes, but stood aside to let him pass through. Wishyouwas glanced back at Penny and nodded before going in.

The guards aimed their spears at Penny once more.

'Sorry,' she said. 'We *have* to do this.'

Fragile's face scrunched up. 'Do what?'

The whole front gate creaked open. Wishyouwas dangled from the entry rope on the other side.

For a split second the guards didn't know how to react. Before they made up their minds Penny barged past them, gathered up Wishyouwas and ran.

15

Sounding the Alarm

A sleepy silence filled the Sorters' tunnel. The lights were dimmed, flickering off the posters on the walls. The furniture was shuttered or closed. Instead of bustle and rush, the air was hushed and still. Penny's worries grew as she realised it was still early for the nocturnal Sorters. She needed Their Highnesses to be awake – to listen! She ducked beneath empty ropes and raced with Wishyouwas through the quiet avenue of letterboxes until they reached the postbox.

Penny hid the lock picker in her satchel, while

Wishyouwas yanked on the watch chain dangling from the letter slot. Almost at once Stampduty's pen-nib nose appeared. His eyes narrowed to slits as he stared first at Penny, then at Wishyouwas.

'What is the meaning of this?' he demanded. 'Where are the guards? Why is this human inside The Bureau *again*?'

'It's urgent!' Penny answered. 'We need to speak to Their Highnesses right away!'

Stampduty's yellow pencil poked out of the letter slot. 'Then you will have to wait. The next Audience is not until—'

'There isn't time!' Penny said.

She heard creaks behind her, and turned to see many ruffled heads and moon-bright eyes peeking out of the letterboxes. Fragile and Handlewithcare bounded over, their faces creased into furious scowls.

'The human broke in!' they snarled.

'You have to believe me,' Penny said to Stampduty. 'It's a matter of life and death!'

'The next Audience is not scheduled until four

o'clock,' Stampduty insisted, tapping his pencil against the collection times.

With a swift leap Wishyouwas jumped off Penny's shoulder, snatched the pencil out of Stampduty's grasp and landed on the ground. 'We is not waiting!' he squeaked.

The pupils of Stampduty's eyes turned to pinpricks. 'Guards!' he cried. 'Summon all the Sorters. Let us see what Their Highnesses make of *this*!'

Wishyouwas fiddled with the pencil as the Sorters assembled in dribs and drabs, forming a ragged semicircle and rubbing sleep from their eyes. Penny bit her lip, wishing they would hurry up. Finally Dearsir and Dearmadam waddled out of the postbox and sat in their inkwells, their faces even more pinched and severe than usual. They glared at Penny as Stampduty announced: 'Unscheduled Audience in session! All rise for Their Highnesses Dearsir and Dearmadam, Supreme Rulers of the Sorters of The Bureau, Keepers of—'

'Yes, yes!' croaked Dearsir, waving his paw. 'Let us get on with it, for parcel's sake, so we can rest.' He scowled at Penny. 'So, human, you have returned! Why do you insist on ruining our peace?'

Penny took a deep breath. 'I know you told me not to come back,' she said, 'and I wouldn't have, but Withlove was trapped at my uncle's post office!'

'Very well, send a rescue party,' ordered Dearsir. 'Give Stampduty the address of the post office.'

'No – she's not there any more. Now the rat catcher has got her!' Penny said. 'And that's not all. He's taking rats out of the sewers and using a postbox to send them into the tunnels.'

Dearmadam raised her paw. 'Please slow down. Do you mean to tell us that somebody is setting rats loose on *purpose*?'

Penny nodded. 'I saw a map in his van, with a circle around Mount Pleasant. And he tried to make the Postmaster General close the railway tonight – so that he could *catch* rats, he said. But it's a lie. I think he wants the railway shut so that he can release even *more* rats.'

She expected Their Highnesses to look frightened, or at least worried, but Dearmadam simply twitched her nose. 'Even if this were true,' she said, 'why would a rat catcher *release* rats into the tunnels? That is the opposite of his duty!'

Penny looked at the small, confused faces all around her and hated what she had to say next. But she had to make them understand. 'He said the best way to catch a rat is with another rat ... I think he's using them to get *you*.'

Fear rippled through the listening Sorters. They shifted on their paws, speaking in scared whispers.

'Who is this rat catcher you speak of?' demanded Dearsir.

Penny swallowed. 'His name's Stanley Scrawl.'

Thiswayup gave a funny jerk and toppled off his crutch.

'Your Highnesses,' said Stampduty, pointing a long, bony finger at Penny. 'How do we know the girl has not informed this rat catcher about us? She could be trying to frighten us out into the open, where we can be caught.'

'That's not true!' Penny said, her cheeks burning.

'Dear Penny wouldn't never betray us!' Wishyouwas said.

'I most certainly agree!' huffed Thiswayup, heaving himself back on his paws. 'Your Highnesses, I must say—'

'Dear Penny is right.' Posthaste, the broadshouldered Deliverer, stepped forwards. He gave her a quick nod. 'We need to protect ourselves. The heap outside the front gate is only designed to trick a human's gaze. It will not fool the rats. The Bureau will draw them in with the promise of food and warmth. We have encountered enough of them already to know what threat they pose to us.'

'Scrawl caught Withlove for a reason,' Penny insisted. 'He's planning something tonight. I know it. It'll be safer if you leave now.'

'Leave?' spluttered Dearsir.

'How dare you suggest such a thing!' said Dearmadam, glowering at Penny. 'It has taken generations to create our world, ruled by discipline and duty.' She faced the Sorters and lifted her nose.

'We cannot risk trusting this human or any others by exposing ourselves. The rats are a lesser danger. If they come, we shall deal with them.'

'Your Highnesses!' called out Thiswayup, raising his paw. 'Please listen to me. I *must* warn you—'

But before he could finish his sentence, Their Highnesses, Wishyouwas and the other Sorters darted their eyes in the direction of the front gate, their ears twitching.

A moment later Penny heard a distant, high-pitched siren reverberate through the tunnel walls. The long wail rose up, fell, then rose again.

'Bless my stamps,' muttered Thiswayup, clutching his compass. 'I haven't heard that since the war.'

'What is it?' Penny asked in a frightened whisper.

Thiswayup looked up at her, his fur paling even whiter. 'It is the humans' emergency alarm, Dear Penny. It means the railway is being evacuated.'

16

Fight or Flight

Thiswayup hobbled off in a hurry. The rest of the Sorters clustered closer together, staring along the tunnel and clutching their ears as the shrill siren echoed. None of them seemed to know what to do.

'It may only be a test alarm,' said Dearsir, raising his voice. 'Nevertheless, we shall upgrade our Threat Level. Stampduty, read out the Urgency Procedures.'

A Sorter scurried on to the scales and dropped another weight on top, swinging the dial around to 'Urgent'.

Stampduty rifled through his notebook. 'Guards are to protect the front gate and report back any disturbances,' he announced. Fragile and Handlewithcare scampered away.

'I will join them,' said Posthaste. He ran off, followed by a handful of other burly-looking Deliverers.

'No Sorters are permitted in or out of The Bureau until further notice,' Stampduty continued.

'But what about Withlove?' Penny said. 'She's still out there!'

'We shall rescue her when it is safe to do so,' replied Dearmadam. 'You too need to remain here for the time being, girl.'

Uncle Frank will think I'm missing! Penny thought. But then she remembered – he was here somewhere, at Mount Pleasant! If she could reach him and make him believe her about the Sorters, he might be able to help!

While Stampduty continued reading through the procedures, Penny knelt and whispered, 'Wishyouwas, can you help me get out again?'

He nodded and pointed behind Their Highnesses' postbox. 'There is a back gate, Dear Penny,' he said. 'But we never uses it.'

Penny considered the curtain of mail sacks with the Queen's portrait pinned to it. If she could somehow sneak behind it …

'Your Highnesses!' Posthaste bounded back, his watch-dial medallion bumping against his chest. 'I am afraid to report that rats are already outside the front gate. A giant swarm.'

His words struck guilt into Penny's heart, all thoughts of leaving through the back gate forgotten. What if she and Wishyouwas had led the rats here without meaning to? She had to stay. She had to help stop them!

As if he could read her mind, Wishyouwas jumped on to her shoulder. Without waiting to hear what Their Highnesses would say, Penny ran through the letterbox avenue, past the side tunnel and under the ropes. As they rounded the final bend and saw the front gate, Wishyouwas's toes curled under him.

Penny saw sharp claws poking through the horizontal letter slot. Fragile and Handlewithcare braced themselves in front of the petrol hatch, their muscles tensed and spears poised as it rattled and shook. Over the wail of the siren, Penny heard a frantic scrabbling coming from behind it, like the *scritch-scratch* of dry pen nibs.

With a patter of paws Posthaste and other Deliverers leaped past Penny to form a semicircle around the hatch. They grasped a hurriedly gathered arsenal of pens, letter openers and rubber-band slingshots loaded with drawing pins. Wishyouwas jumped down and joined ranks, clutching the pencil he'd taken from Stampduty. Penny looked around for anything she could use as a weapon, but the Sorters' furniture was still shuttered. All she could see nearby was a pile of useless parcel boxes stuffed with wastepaper.

The hatch juddered. The Sorters' ears flattened, their knuckles bone-white as they gripped their weapons. Would it hold?

The answer came almost at once. The metal hatch buckled inwards, creating a thin gap at the side. A whiskery nose poked through. The Sorters launched an instant hail of drawing pins at the hatch. The rat screeched and jerked back, but only for a moment. Another nose poked through and long yellow teeth gnashed. Penny darted forwards and pressed her heels against the hatch, forcing it shut. Her skin crawled as she felt claws and teeth scratching on the other side.

Her eyes fell once more on the parcel boxes. 'Build a wall!' she said, pointing at them.

'Good idea,' agreed Posthaste. 'Work together! Half of us build, the other half keep watch.'

A dozen Sorters sprang into action, dragging and pushing box after box up to Penny. She rammed one against the petrol hatch, then mounted others on top and at the sides. The guards kept a close eye in case any rats made it through.

Messages passed swiftly down the tunnel. Sorters unlocked cupboards and shelving units. A line of helpers began to straggle to the gate, wobbling beneath the weight of books, boxes and anything else they could carry. Penny hauled everything into a higher and higher heap and the Sorters bound it all together with ropes severed from the tunnel ceiling.

'What are you doing?' a shrill voice demanded, making Penny jump. Stampduty, Dearsir and Dearmadam wheeled up to them inside a wicker trolley.

'Stop this at once!' ordered Dearsir, trembling with indignation. 'This is not in the Urgency Procedures!'

'The rats are trying to break through!' Penny said, out of breath.

By now the front gate was hidden from sight. 'The only one I can see breaking anything is you!' Dearmadam said.

'Return every item to its proper place,' ordered Stampduty, scribbling in his notebook. 'As per Rule Ten, Section One of the …' He stopped as a ripping sound came from the wall of boxes. He peered over the edge of the trolley, a brand-new yellow pencil hovering in mid-air.

Penny whirled round.

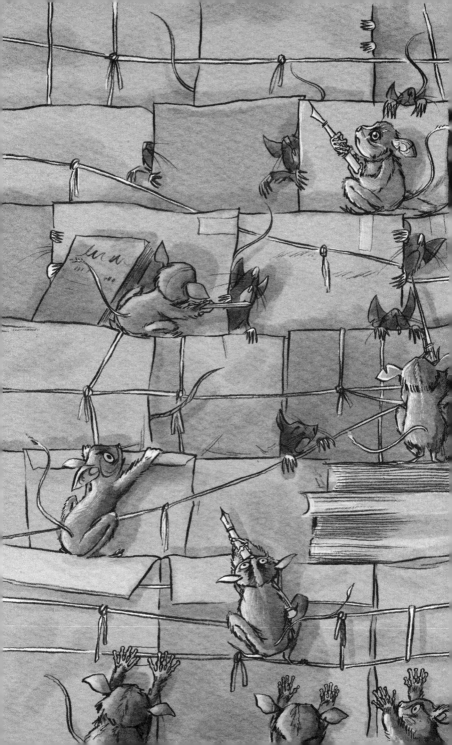

A small hole had appeared in a box at the bottom. An oily black head squirmed out of it, followed by half of a fat, sleek body.

Handlewithcare leaped forwards and stabbed at the rat with his fountain pen.

'The rats are eating their way through!' cried Penny.

'Form a line of defence!' commanded Fragile. 'Any Sorters without weapons, fall back!'

The armed Sorters hopped into a row before the wall, while the others fell behind Penny in disordered huddles. Their moonlike eyes were dark-rimmed with fear.

Another rat poked through and the guards fought it back. A different box tore open, and then a third. The guards formed three teams, one in front of each hole. They took turns to lunge forwards as one by one the hungry, desperate rats tried to wriggle inside. Fragile roared, and stabbed a particularly ferocious one in the ear with his letter opener.

'We'll never stop them!' Penny said. 'There are too many. You have to leave!'

'We cannot leave,' insisted Dearsir. 'It would risk everything we have built!'

'There's no choice,' Penny said. '*Please*, you have to go!'

'But this is our home,' said a Solver close by, clutching his monocle.

'Where *will* we go?' asked a female Deliverer.

'I don't know,' Penny said. Then she remembered the lift that led to the car park. 'Wait, I do! Wishyouwas and I know a way out. We can show you!'

'Follow them!' bellowed Handlewithcare, jabbing his fountain pen at a gigantic rat twice his size. 'We'll hold them off as long as we can. *Run!*'

17

The Trap

Leaving a line of guards to protect the wall, the other Sorters scurried away, scattering in all directions.

'I'll open the back gate!' Penny told Wishyouwas.

He nodded. 'I is delivering the message, Dear Penny.' He began zigzagging across the tunnel, directing the other Sorters where to go.

Penny glanced at Their Highnesses and grabbed hold of their wicker trolley. 'Sorry!' she said, ignoring their protests.

She shoved the trolley past the ransacked

cupboards and shelves. Furry bodies brushed her legs and jumped over her shoes, streaming past her. But when Penny reached the side tunnel, she noticed the Sorters split off and scamper down there instead of heading to the back gate.

'Where are you going?' she shouted. 'That's the wrong way!'

'They are saving the lost letters,' Stampduty sniffed from inside the trolley. 'That is a Sorter's first duty.'

'Tell them to come back!' Penny said. Then she stopped herself, realising deep down she could never convince them. She knew how much letters meant to the Sorters. Wishyouwas had risked his life every day to gather them. They would *never* leave them behind.

She heard Thiswayup's reassuring voice rise above the clamour of scurrying paws, fluttering paper and panicked squeaks. He was standing on a parcel box at the side of the tunnel, struggling to stay upright as he waved his compass to direct a straggle of old, sick and more feeble Sorters towards the end of the tunnel. Some were white-furred and frail, others had bandaged limbs or carried babies no bigger than Penny's thumb. 'This way!' he called over the din. 'Hurry now, that's right. Don't panic, we shall all be safe soon.'

Penny pushed the trolley up to him.

'Thank parcels, Dear Penny!' he said. 'Please, help as many as you can. Take these as well.' He tapped the box he stood on. 'My hang-gliders. We may need them!'

After lifting Thiswayup into the trolley, Penny opened her satchel and filled it with as many hang-gliders from the box as would fit. Then she swerved the trolley between the avenue of letterboxes, using it like a lifeboat to gather the Sorters who couldn't keep up. It was full, and twice as heavy, by the time she reached Their Highnesses' postbox.

She pulled aside the curtain behind it, scrunching up the paper portrait of the Queen, to reveal a round metal door marked FLOOD GATE. It had a wheel in the middle like the kind she imagined on a bank vault. Penny heaved on it, but it didn't budge.

The Sorters gathered around her feet, clutching a variety of white and brown envelopes in their paws and mouths. Several leaped on to the wheel, adding their weight to help. The wheel began to crank round with a grinding, rusty squeal.

Penny jumped as a colossal crash sounded from up the tunnel, followed by the distant cries of the guards.

'*The wall has fallen!*'

Penny glanced over her shoulder and the breath rushed out of her.

The rats had broken through. The guards backed down the tunnel, while beyond them appeared a thick black line – a wriggling, screeching mass of rats.

The guards were jumping and leaping fast, holding them at bay with their weapons. The rats' teeth bared and their claws scratched as they tried

to writhe past the defenders. Penny knew they were almost out of time.

She gritted her teeth and strained on the wheel with all her strength. With a groan it finally gave way, and the evacuation siren swelled in her ears as the back gate swung open.

'Dear Penny!' Wishyouwas hopped on to her shoulder. 'Follow me!'

Penny bumped the trolley through the opening into the darkness of the tunnel. She had to leave the gate open for the guards to escape. With little light to see by, she trusted Wishyouwas's directions as he squeaked urgently in her ear. Around them the lost letters sounded like rustling leaves and the Sorters' eyes blinked like stars as they scampered all around her. The trolley bumped and jolted between the rails. Penny's lungs burned and the strength began to seep from her legs.

Just as she thought she couldn't go on, a thin crescent of light appeared ahead. She gasped in relief. A deserted platform came into view, almost identical to the one she'd seen before, with a control office and a driverless red train resting motionless on the tracks.

The Sorters leaped on to the platform and Penny heaved up the trolley. The rats followed them from the mouth of the tunnel, just a trickle at first. Fragile, Handlewithcare and the few remaining defenders lined up at the edge of the platform, their fur dark with sweat, fighting any rats that tried to climb up.

Wishyouwas leaped off Penny's shoulder and ran along the platform, then stopped and scurried back. 'Dear Penny!' he squeaked. 'We has to run!'

But Penny knew she couldn't run fast enough to escape the rats. Not with the trolley as well. She looked at the train and Scrawl's words came back to her, from when she had ridden in his van. *You'd have to be as fast as a* train *to outrun them* ...

Thiswayup touched her hand. 'I see we have the same idea, Dear Penny. If you carry me into the control office, I can operate it.'

Penny nodded. 'Get on the train!' she shouted across the platform. She carried Thiswayup inside a room containing a bank of dials, switches and levers beneath a map of the railway. 'We have to get to the garage,' she told him. 'We can get up to the car park that way.' Thiswayup rubbed his paws together and began twiddling levers.

Penny raced outside to the platform. The Sorters were helping each other climb into the carriages. She lifted those still in the trolley, including Their Highnesses, who hunkered down among the mail sacks without complaint.

The train clanked and rolled forwards. The rats scattered at the sudden motion. Penny raced to get Thiswayup, then returned and ran alongside the train, grabbing hold and jumping into the first carriage, where the Sorters had left space for her.

'Quick!' she called.

Fragile, Handlewithcare and the guards dropped their blood-tipped weapons. They took flying leaps, landing in the rear carriages a fraction before the train rocketed into the tunnel.

Penny braced her arms against the sides of the cramped carriage as they hurtled through the

narrow, winding darkness, wind rippling through her hair and the Sorters' fur. The train bumped and jolted, and lost letters fluttered, almost whipping out of their paws.

The train wheels sparked and in the flashes of light she saw the Sorters' exhausted but relieved faces as they clung on to the sacks.

Penny let herself breathe. Scrawl's plan was in shreds! The Sorters might be homeless and battle-scarred, but they were safe from the rats for now.

Her mind raced ahead, trying to think of where they would go once they reached the car park. There shouldn't be too many people about at this late hour. The smog would help hide them too ...

The train swung to the left, travelling in a long loop. As it straightened, the speed lessened and they passed a sign with an arrow that read MAINTENANCE GARAGE. A circle of light appeared up ahead and grew brighter. Fluorescent ceiling lights dazzled Penny's vision and the train slowed, then rattled to a stop.

Before her eyes had time to adjust, Penny sensed the Sorters beside her stiffen.

A dark shadow fell over them. Penny looked up and recoiled. A snouted gas mask leered down at her and two huge hands holding a sack lunged forwards.

'No!' she yelled, as Stanley Scrawl swooped the sack over her head.

18

All for One

Through the sack Penny heard Ripper growling and snapping his jaws, amid the Sorters' terrified squeaks. The guards had left their weapons behind on the platform. Scrawl had even snatched Penny's satchel away, with the lock picker and hanggliders inside – they were defenceless against the greyhound!

'Get inside the workshop, all of you!' Scrawl's voice hissed through the gas mask. 'Ripper'll tear you to pieces if you run!'

Penny struggled, desperate to help them, but her

187

wrists were tied behind her back with parcel tape. Scrawl shoved her forwards across a concrete surface, before pushing her to sit on the floor. A door slammed, the sound of the siren dimmed and she heard a key being turned in a lock. A moment later the sack was yanked off her head.

She blinked and coughed in the bright lights of a workshop. The pungent smell of oil, sweat and fear stung her nostrils. Hammers and crowbars, note-pads and pencils were strewn over a long table, abandoned in the earlier rush to evacuate the railway. Massive machinery lined the walls, still humming with power. Ripper growled and herded the Sorters into a tight circle in the middle of the floor. The smallest Sorters clutched on to their parents, their tiny bodies trembling.

Penny spotted Wishyouwas. He tried to dart towards her, but Ripper snapped at his head, forcing him to hop back.

Scrawl thumped from the door to stand before the Sorters, towering over them. He held Penny's satchel in one fist and peeled off his gas mask with

the other. He tossed both into a corner, before spreading his arms out like a circus ringmaster.

'Salutations!' he said, the corners of his mouth curling upwards. 'My name is Stanley Scrawl. Enjoy your little ride, did you? I knew you'd have to take this route to escape, but having the lot of you parcelled up on the train was a lovely bonus – made it so much easier to round you up!'

Penny felt sick and hollow inside. Scrawl hadn't wanted the rats to *kill* the Sorters, only drive them out so he could catch them himself! He must have known she knew about them from the start, and let her lead them straight to him. It was all her fault.

'Please let them go!' she pleaded. 'They've done nothing wrong!'

'One more word from you and I'll tape your mouth shut!' Scrawl snapped. He paced around the circle of Sorters in his hobnailed boots, narrowly missing their paws and tails. The Sorters' fearful eyes followed him. 'You don't remember me, do you?' he said. 'Let me remind you.' He dug inside a voluminous pocket of his long brown overcoat and pulled out a peaked postman's cap with a gold badge, which he jammed on to his head.

'Once,' he said, 'I was the most respected postman in London. My speciality was finding missing letters. During the war people would pay almost *anything* for me to track them down a letter that had got lost – a message from a sweetheart in France, perhaps, a letter from a beloved child sent away to the country, money sent to a poor relative made homeless in the bombings ...' He sniffed. 'People always welcomed old Stan coming along the street.'

He jabbed his fingernail at the Sorters. 'Until one of *you* sneaked into my van and took a valuable missing letter that I'd held on to for safe keeping. The next day, the Postmaster General ordered me into his office. He held up that same letter, together with a little anonymous note. He accused me of stealing post – *me*, the best postman in London! So ... which one of you was it who sent him that message?'

From another of his pockets, Scrawl plucked out

the little white stick Penny had seen in his van. He bent low and dangled it above the Sorters' heads, raking his eyes over them. With creeping horror Penny realised it was a leg bone – which could only mean …

Tap, tap, tap. Thiswayup hobbled between the Sorters to stand at the front. He lifted his white, wrinkled head and faced Scrawl. 'It was *I* who uncovered what you were really doing, Stanley Scrawl,' he said.

Penny caught her breath as shocked whispers broke out among the Sorters. Scrawl clubbed his fists. Penny tried to wriggle to her feet, but Ripper leaped in front of her and growled, baring his teeth until she sat back down.

The old Solver gripped his compass, only wobbling slightly. 'I am only sorry I did not discover your crime sooner. You hid other people's letters, waiting until they became desperate enough to pay you to find what was rightfully theirs! Your greed only heaped *more* misery on people during the darkest days of all.'

Scrawl's nose wrinkled. 'It never hurt people to wait a few extra weeks, did it? They always got their letters in the end. After all, "absence makes the heart grow fonder". It was a win-win situation. But *you*,' he sneered, 'stole *everything* from me. I lost my job, my money and my reputation. So who's the real thief?'

'Your quarrel is with me alone,' replied Thiswayup. 'Let the others go free. They had no part in this.'

'I want my fair share. All for one,' replied Scrawl. 'In return for all the years you cost me. First I clawed my way back into the Royal Mail, begging for a job as a rat catcher. Ripper tracked you down to the tunnels, thanks to this.' He wiggled Thiswayup's leg bone. 'I've waited a long time, planning how to flush you all out, waiting for an opportunity. Then the smog came along, giving me the perfect excuse. And close to Christmas too …' He straightened and pulled a watch from one of his pockets. 'But now your time's up.' He cast his eyes over the rest of the Sorters. 'Which one of you's the leader?'

Don't tell him! Penny thought. But on cue Stampduty pointed to Dearsir and Dearmadam. 'You will address Their Highnesses, Dearsir and Dearmadam, Supreme Rulers of—'

'A-ha!' Scrawl thumped over to where Their Highnesses crouched. Penny could see their jowls trembling, but though Scrawl was a hundred times their size, they held their noses high. She felt a newfound respect for them.

Scrawl leaned down and poked his sharp finger-nail at Dearsir's belly. 'Now listen very carefully.' He pointed at the workshop door. 'Out there in the garage is a train stuffed full of Christmas post.' He aimed his finger at Penny. 'The girl is going to carry in the sacks, and you're going to sort through the letters and cards, every single last one, and take out anything valuable you find. I want it all.'

Dearsir gaped at him. 'We do not steal!'

'It is the Law of the Letter!' Dearmadam added.

Scrawl lifted his boot, and for a sickening moment Penny thought he would squash them flat. But instead he thumped his foot down on the ground and burst into laughter. '"The Law of the Letter"!' he hooted. 'That's a good one!' He strode across the room to a machine with a metal funnel at the top and pressed a button. Rotating teeth sliced around at high speed and thin slivers of paper spewed out into a wicker trolley. 'You follow *my* law now,' he said.

But little Yourstruly with the stuck-up quiff, whom Penny had seen in the school, hopped up in the air and squeaked, 'Sorters – never – steal!'

'That's right!' spoke up a Solver.

'We never have and we never will!' cried an elderly Deliverer.

All the Sorters echoed the call: '*Sorters never steal!*'

Scrawl's mouth twitched with amusement. 'Let me make my message loud and clear.' He thrust his hand inside another pocket of his overcoat and yanked out a small bundle of fur, bound with parcel string.

'Withlove!' Penny cried above the alarmed

squeaks of the Sorters. The tiny Gatherer wriggled and writhed, trying to move her strong back legs.

Scrawl dangled Withlove above the funnel of the shredder by the tip of her tail. 'If you won't do what I want,' he said to the Sorters with a shrug, 'then this is what's going to happen.' He began to lower her into the funnel, towards the whirring blades.

'We agree!' said Dearsir at once.

Scrawl yanked Withlove up again with a smirk. He switched off the shredder, stuffed Withlove back inside his pocket, then looked at Penny. 'Start bringing those sacks in. And if you even *think* about running, say goodbye to your special little friend.'

It took Penny a moment to realise Scrawl's mistake – he thought Withlove was Wishyouwas. He had no idea Wishyouwas was still in the crowd, keeping his eyes locked on Penny.

Scrawl threw open the workshop door. 'Get to work!'

19

Sorters Never Steal

The Sorters formed a long chain, their faces lowered with shame. Felicitations gathered her tiny pupils around her in a huddle at the back, murmuring to them softly.

The Sorters forced themselves to open the Christmas post and the rustling of paper soon filled the workshop. Penny couldn't meet their eyes as she went back and forth between them and the train outside. Everything she'd done had hurt them – Wishyouwas had been downgraded, Withlove had been caught, and now all the Sorters had fallen into

Scrawl's trap. They were right not to trust humans, she thought.

She grabbed a sack and struggled to pull it out of the carriage. After she dragged it into the workshop, the Gatherers untied it and passed the cards and letters it contained down the chain to the Solvers. They felt along the edges of each item, just as Thiswayup had checked if Penny's letter was a High Value Envelope. They either nodded and passed them along to the Deliverers, who emptied the valuables into a sack, or shook their heads and sent the non-HIVE items back up the line to be placed in a pile. Penny noticed Stampduty scribbling furiously with a pencil on a scrap of paper he must have sneaked down from the worktable, though she couldn't think why. How could the Sorters' rules help them now?

While Ripper guarded the doorway, Scrawl moved to stand beside the shredder, twirling the workshop key on his fingernail and watching the Sorters with the keen eyes of a vulture. Unexpectedly he marched up to the Deliverers, trampling over

their neat piles of opened envelopes, and shoved his hand inside one of the sacks they had been filling. Penny paused to watch. His fist came out clenching postal orders and crisp bank notes.

'Just checking you're not up to any tricks,' he said, then noticed Penny staring. 'What are you looking at?' he said. 'Get back to work!'

Penny went out of the workshop with the faintest flicker of an idea. She checked Scrawl wasn't looking in her direction, then peered around the garage. The space was enormous, criss-crossed with tracks where trains came to be mended and maintained.

There! At the far end she spotted the gated lift that she and Wishyouwas had ridden in. If she could only reach it and find Uncle Frank, she could make him send a rescue party. But to do *that* she needed enough time to get away from Scrawl, without putting Withlove and the Sorters in even greater danger …

No. Penny snuffed the idea out. What if it went wrong? She'd already done enough harm to the

Sorters. She kept her head down and dragged another sack inside the workshop.

'Move faster!' Scrawl bawled at the Sorters, pacing before them. He stopped and leaned over Felicitations and her pupils. The teacher ushered the tiny Sorters behind her.

'Why aren't you working?' he demanded.

'They are far too young,' insisted Felicitations, 'especially for this terrible work.'

'*Everyone* works!' Scrawl snatched the sack from Penny's grasp. He tore off the label, tipped it up and dumped the contents on the pupils' tiny heads. Their smothered squeaks and squeals could just be heard as Sorters leaped over to unbury them.

Penny's whole body shook with anger. She couldn't let him bully them this way. To hide the look on her face she hurried outside to fetch another sack, her mind racing back to the plan she'd squashed moments ago. She *had* to try.

As she re-entered the workshop she located Wishyouwas and caught his eye. He stood in the chain of Gatherers, passing along envelopes. His ears twitched towards her, silently letting her know he was ready to help.

Penny took a deep breath. The other Sorters would hate her for what she was about to say. She was relying on it. But she couldn't bear it if she lost Wishyouwas's trust.

Gathering her fury into the pit of her stomach, she dropped the sack to the ground with a thump. 'I won't do any more!' she shouted, stamping her foot for good measure. 'It's not fair. I helped you and now you're treating me the same as them!'

Scrawl stopped pacing. He turned and stomped across the workshop towards her. 'Get back to work!' he ordered.

Penny stood straight. 'Not until you give me that creature you've got. All I ever wanted was a pet.' She crossed her fingers behind her back. 'I told my uncle to put the cage you gave me on the door to try and catch it, but you took it first!'

The Sorters paused in their work and stared at her, their eyes round and disbelieving.

Scrawl stooped over Penny. His breath smelt

putrid. 'Nice try!' he said, patting the pocket with Withlove inside. 'But I can do this with or without your help.'

'No you can't,' argued Penny. 'Without me you wouldn't have caught them at all. They would have stayed and fought the rats rather than leave. You don't understand them like I do. It was *me* who convinced them to escape. It was *me* who told them to get on to the train …'

She glanced at the Sorters. All along the chain their fur darkened as if a cloud had swept over them. Their Highnesses' jowls trembled with indignation. One by one they turned away from her, their ears and eyes cast down as they slowly and methodically went back to sorting the stolen post. Wishyouwas frowned, still darting looks between her and Scrawl. Had he believed her treachery too?

Penny felt a tear slide down her cheek. She wiped it away, hoping Scrawl would put it down to her tantrum. 'But now you've trapped them all, I'll never have the chance to catch one again!' she cried.

'Let me have one. I don't care which. I only want one to keep.'

Scrawl's eyes became thin slits as he considered. 'All right,' he sniffed at last. 'I'm a fair man. After you've brought in all the sacks, you can have *one*.'

'Thank you!' Penny forced herself to smile at him. 'Can I choose now? *Please*. I'll go extra fast afterwards, I promise! *Please* can I?'

Scrawl's lip curled. 'Only if it'll shut you up. Go on then – make it fast!'

He returned to guard the shredder while Penny moved towards the Sorters, who shuffled away from her. She bent down, pretending to inspect them.

'Take a small one!' ordered Scrawl.

There were squeaks of protest as grown-up Sorters clutched their babies.

'What about this one?' Penny knelt beside Thiswayup, who was feeling the edges of a letter without meeting her gaze. 'It's already injured anyway.'

'No!' Scrawl said, a horrible smirk on his face. 'I've got plans for *that* one.'

As Penny stood, she said to Thiswayup in a rushed whisper, '*Nothing is ever lost that cannot be solved!*'

Thiswayup peeped up at her, his misty eyes shining.

'Fight back!' Penny said under her breath. 'Wait for my signal. Pass on the message!'

Thiswayup gave the tiniest nod. He hobbled to the next Solver and began murmuring in their ear.

Penny continued down the line, towards the Gatherers. 'Um …' she wondered loudly, to cover the sound of the Sorters whispering her message. She stooped again. 'I want this one!' she said, lifting Wishyouwas in her hands. She could feel his back paws bunching, preparing to spring away. Then his paw curled round her little finger. She tried not to smile as his trust made her swell with hope. 'This one's injured too. Look.' She held him out.

'Let me see,' said Scrawl.

'Here,' Penny said, pointing. 'Its tail's damaged.'

Scrawl left the shredder and came up close. His long nose lowered towards Wishyouwas …

'Now!' Penny shouted. She opened her hands and Wishyouwas leaped on to Scrawl's nose, yanking it hard.

Scrawl yelled and stumbled backwards. He swiped his hand at his face, hitting his own nose as Wishyouwas dropped inside his collar and crawled into his overcoat.

'Get off!' Scrawl screeched, his body writhing.

Ripper barked and ran around his master, snapping the air while Scrawl whirled in circles. He flailed and flapped, trying to shake Wishyouwas out.

The other Sorters sprang into action. Furry bodies flew through the air, leaping on to Scrawl's arms and legs.

Scrawl roared. He wriggled out of his overcoat and threw it to the floor. Penny dived on it to search for Withlove, but it was Wishyouwas who found her first, tied up and trembling, and bit the string off.

The Sorters darted around Scrawl's boots, leaping out of reach as he stamped and lunged, trying to catch another one.

Meanwhile Penny ran for the table. Grabbing a handful of discarded tools, she sprinted for the shredder and stuffed hammers, spanners and screwdrivers inside the funnel, then pressed the button.

The machine gave a loud metallic groan, the rotating teeth snapped, and it coughed out a puff of black smoke.

'You lying brat!' Scrawl's teeth jutted in a snarl. He twisted towards the doorway and Penny's stomach lurched. He still had the key – he'd lock them all in!

Several Sorters tried to run outside, but Ripper leaped in their path, jaws snapping. They formed a ragged line, shielding themselves with flimsy envelopes. Penny looked for Wishyouwas and spotted him by her satchel in the corner, wriggling inside it.

By now Scrawl was almost at the door. Not knowing what else to do, Penny grabbed a box of pencils on the table and hurled it across the workshop. They littered the ground around Scrawl's feet, rolling under his boots. Scrawl yelled as he skidded and crashed to the ground, half in and half out of the doorway. The nearest Sorters sprang on to the pencils, clutching them as weapons.

'Go, Dear Penny!' cried Thiswayup, waving his arm. 'Find help!'

'I can't leave you all!' she said.

'You must – it is the only way.'

Scrawl grunted and rolled over.

Wishyouwas jumped on Penny's shoulder, clutching something in his paw. 'We has to go!' he squeaked.

Penny leaped over Scrawl, diving through the doorway. She turned and sprinted through the garage towards the lift. Ripper barked madly behind her, then she heard a *slam!*

Scrawl's laugh echoed. 'No way out now,' he jeered.

Penny looked over her shoulder – Scrawl was turning the key in the workshop door, shutting the Sorters on the other side. She reached the lift and pulled on the gate, but it didn't budge. 'It's locked!'

'Of course it is,' Scrawl said as he stalked

forwards. 'Didn't think I'd let you run off too, did you?'

But Wishyouwas sprang on to the gate and opened his paw to reveal Penny's lock picker. He twiddled it in the keyhole.

'Oi!' Scrawl's boots chopped towards them.

'Quickly, Wishyouwas!' Penny gasped.

Wishyouwas's paws were a blur, until Penny heard a *click*. She wrenched open the gate, flew inside and shut it again, straight on to Scrawl's clutching fingers. He howled in pain and snatched his hand back.

Wishyouwas had already leaped on to the control panel and pushed a button. The lift juddered and rose upwards.

Scrawl's sweating face pressed against the gate, his eyes dark pits of hatred. 'You haven't seen the last of me!' he snarled. Then he was gone.

20

The Meeting

Penny jabbed the lift button, willing it to move faster. *What will Scrawl do to the rest of the Sorters?* she worried.

As soon as the lift stopped she opened the gate and they rushed into the cold night air. But instead of an empty car park, a huge crowd of Royal Mail workers milled among the vehicles, stamping their feet for warmth and sharing flasks of steaming tea. Wishyouwas slid down Penny's back and hid inside her coat pocket.

'I'll look for my uncle,' Penny said under her breath. 'He must be here somewhere.'

She spotted a curly-haired lady standing on the bonnet of a van, wearing a bright yellow jacket with EVACUATION WARDEN printed on it. 'The Fire Brigade are on their way to help with the rats,' she announced through the long metal funnel of a megaphone. 'They're taking a bit longer to reach us due to the smog. Keep close together and stay warm …'

Several people stared at Penny as she squeezed between them. 'Excuse me!' She waved at the warden.

'Goodness me!' The warden lowered her megaphone and leaned down. 'Where have you come from? Are you lost?'

Penny shook her head. 'There's an emergency! I need to find my Uncle Frank—'

'We already know there's an emergency! Why do you think we're outside, freezing our toes off? But I'll find him for you, don't worry.' She stood up again and called over everyone's heads: 'Attention please! I have a young girl here looking for Uncle

Frank.' She peered down again. 'What's your name, love?'

'Penelope!' cried a voice. The sea of people parted and Penny braced herself as Uncle Frank hobbled forwards on his stick. His amber eyes blazed – but to her surprise he slid an arm around her shoulder. 'Are you all right?' he asked. 'Why the devil are you here?'

Before Penny could explain, a stern voice she recognised called out, 'What is going on?' A tall man marched through the crowd. He resembled a pencil, with his striped suit and clipped grey hair. Penny knew he was the Postmaster General before she even saw his flashing gold badge. He glared down at her.

'She's ma niece, sir,' explained Uncle Frank hurriedly.

'Your niece? This is a restricted area. Escort her home at once. A postmaster of your rank should know better!'

'Aye, sir,' Uncle Frank said, turning the colour of a postbox.

The workers glanced at them and began gossiping as the Postmaster General spun on his heel to walk away. But Penny realised he was their best chance to get help for the Sorters. She darted forwards and caught hold of his sleeve.

'Wait, sir!' she said. 'Stanley Scrawl is stealing the Christmas post! He's in the maintenance garage right now!'

The Postmaster General's face was stiff as cardboard. 'And how would you know that, young lady?'

'I'm sorry, sir,' said Uncle Frank, trying to pull Penny away. 'Ma niece is *very* imaginative ...'

'It's true!' Penny insisted, shaking herself free. 'Please, you have to believe me! He's trapped the Sorters!'

The warden standing on the van bonnet said kindly, 'The mail sorters are all out here, love. I've taken a roll call. There's nobody missing.'

'No, that's not what I mean ...' Penny tried to think of how to explain without breaking her promise, but the words wouldn't come. She looked down to see Wishyouwas's head poking out of her pocket. 'They'll never listen!' she whispered. 'I don't know what to do.'

'Come along, Penelope,' sighed Uncle Frank, putting a hand on her back to steer her away. 'I've no idea *how* you got here but I'm taking us home. Then I want an explanation. Ma motorcycle's just – ach!' He snatched his hand away. 'Something nipped me!'

Penny felt paws climbing up her plait, on to her shoulder. 'Wait!' she hissed. 'They'll see you!'

But Wishyouwas emerged into full view, his face set in a determined frown. He puffed himself up, trying to look as big as possible.

'A rat!' shrieked the warden, from above them. Her voice was amplified by the megaphone into a deafening screech.

Wishyouwas's cheeks swelled. 'I is NOT a rat!' he squeaked to the warden. He lifted his chin with a glimmer of his old pride. 'I is a Sorter. Se— Third Class.'

The warden's eyes rolled backwards. She dropped

the megaphone on the bonnet and fainted, straight on top of both the Postmaster General and Uncle Frank.

After that it was chaos.

'Make it say something else!' said a mechanic beside Penny.

'How d'you do it?' asked a postwoman, pushing forwards and trying to poke Wishyouwas. 'Is it a puppet?'

Penny twisted round, trying to find a way out of the grasping hands and prodding fingers.

Wishyouwas wriggled his bottom and jumped high in the air. There was a collective gasp as he landed on the van where the warden had been standing. He struggled to pick up one end of the fallen megaphone. Realising what he wanted to do, Penny shoved through the pressing crowd, jumped on to the bumper and clambered up beside him. Wishyouwas leaped on to her right shoulder. He clutched her plait and Penny's stomach flipped over, but there was no time to be nervous. The Sorters' lives depended on them.

Penny lifted the megaphone to her mouth. 'I have something to say!' she called out.

The crowd suddenly hushed, gazing from her to Wishyouwas in astonishment. Penny took a breath. 'The evacuation was planned by Stanley Scrawl, the Royal Mail rat catcher!' she said. 'He released the rats into the tunnels on purpose. Now he's in the garage, stealing the Christmas post. And he's forcing the Sorters to help him.' She glanced at Wishyouwas. 'The Sorters live in the tunnels and rescue lost letters. They're in terrible danger. You *have* to save them!'

There was silence from the crowd. Penny clenched her trembling hands. It was all for nothing – they still didn't believe her!

Wishyouwas reached his paw for the megaphone and Penny held it in front of him. His chest swelled with air. When he spoke his voice carried through the smog, reaching all corners of Mount Pleasant:

'I is Wishyouwas!' he declared. 'I is a Sorter and Sorters never steal!' Then he recited:

'*The Law of the Letter is written in ink!*
Its rules we obey without stopping to think.
We gather and solve and deliver what's lost,
Without causing trouble or damage or cost.'

Nobody moved. Only blank, gawping faces stared back.

It's no good, Penny thought, her eyes smarting with tears. Nobody would help them!

The Postmaster General broke the stillness. Looking furious and dishevelled from his fall, he marched up to Penny and seized the megaphone, his mouth cemented in a grim line. 'I have seen and heard enough,' he said. He turned to face the workers and raised the megaphone. 'I need volunteers!'

Hundreds of hands shot into the air.

Penny gasped at Wishyouwas. He looked as stunned as she felt.

'Each department form a team,' ordered the Postmaster General. 'Return to the buildings. Seal all the exits. I want Stanley Scrawl apprehended and the stolen letters recovered! And as for the Sorters,' he added, with a quick nod at Wishyouwas, 'bring them all out safely. After all … we are on the same team.'

The workers cheered, their cry echoing across the car park. They quickly split up and scattered in different directions. 'Stay with your uncle,' the Postmaster General said to Penny, before hurrying off, giving orders as he went.

'Well, Penelope,' said Uncle Frank, dusting himself off. 'We have a wee bit of catching up to do!' He lifted his hand for her to climb down, but as she took it, Penny happened to look sideways, towards the end of the car park. Through a swirl of smog she spied a hunched figure dart between two parked vans, shouldering a huge sack. Wishyouwas saw it too and tensed on her shoulder.

'There!' Penny called, but her voice sounded tiny without the megaphone.

'What?' said Uncle Frank, frowning.

'Scrawl – he's getting away!' Penny pointed. 'He must have sneaked out behind the crowd!'

'I is finding him, Dear Penny!' Wishyouwas leaped to the ground and scampered in Scrawl's direction.

'Penelope, wait!' cried Uncle Frank as she slid off the bonnet and sprinted after him. She rushed past motorcycles and vans, struggling to keep Wishyouwas in sight through the smog. 'This way, Dear Penny!' he squeaked from somewhere ahead. 'I has found—'

There was a sharp bark, followed by a panicked squeal.

'Gotcha!' hissed Scrawl, though Penny couldn't see him.

'No!' she cried out.

A door slammed, an engine spluttered to life, and Scrawl's van swerved towards her, dazzling her with its headlamps. Penny fell back as it veered straight past her and out of the car park, vanishing into the night. A sob burst from her chest.

A thunderous growl sounded behind her, and a gleaming red motorcycle drew up, engine purring.

Uncle Frank sat astride it, his stick laid across the handlebars.

'Scrawl has Wishyouwas!' Penny said.

'Climb on!' He chucked her a helmet. 'We can still catch them!' Penny clutched her uncle's jacket and he yanked the accelerator. They surged forwards, ripping the smog to ribbons. Uncle Frank followed Scrawl's deep, swerving tyre tracks in the snow. Penny screwed up her eyes against the icy wind, her clothes rippling with speed as they careered around a corner and sped along the empty streets.

She glimpsed a flash of red tail lights up ahead. Scrawl's van chugged loudly as it swung into a side street.

'Hold tight!' called Uncle Frank, spurring the motorcycle to go faster. They began to gain ground. At the end of the road Scrawl's van screeched and took a sharp corner, clanging into something.

Uncle Frank lowered one leg and twisted the handlebars in the same direction.

Looking ahead, Penny saw Scrawl's van had stopped. Then a figure stepped out from behind it and swung something through the air.

'Duck!' she shouted. Uncle Frank lowered his head and she did too, but a sack clipped the back wheel, sending them into a skid. Penny unbalanced and tipped off into a snowdrift, dragging Uncle Frank with her. The motorcycle smashed into a wall

with an ear-splitting crunch of heavy metal and spinning wheels.

Penny gasped and pulled off her helmet. She heard the rumble of an engine driving away. Checking herself over, she only found a graze on her knee, but her uncle was sprawled like a starfish on the snow, his stick splintered into pieces beside him. She crawled over. 'Uncle Frank!'

'Sorry,' he mumbled. 'Dinna see ... Are you ... all right?'

'Yes, but you're not!'

He closed his eyes and groaned. 'I'm fine ... ma bad leg ... just gimme a sec.'

Penny stood up to look for someone to help, shielding her eyes against the whipping wind and snow. The motorcycle headlamp flickered on and off, lighting up a lopsided postbox and a street sign opposite: SCRIBE'S END.

A jolt of panic coursed through her: Scrawl would vanish into the sewers with Wishyouwas – there was no time! She took off down the dingy alley, slipping and sliding over the icy ground, her arms outstretched in case she fell. She stalked past Scrawl's van, which sat abandoned with the doors open. Then something other than snow crunched beneath her foot. She bent and scooped up a thickly wadded brown envelope, stuffed with cheques and banknotes. She found another further on.

Gritting her teeth, she ran to follow Scrawl's trail.

21
Airmail

Penny hurried deeper into the alley. The smog swirled thicker here, and she slowed as it became more difficult to follow the path of dropped envelopes. She pushed on, until a loud *clang!* from further up the alley made her freeze.

A gust of wind split the smog, and in the brief opening she saw Scrawl crouching at the end of the alley, leaning over the open manhole and pointing a torch down into it. *Her* torch.

Penny forced herself to shuffle forwards, the snow muffling her footsteps.

Every pocket on Scrawl's brown overcoat bulged. So did his sleeves, as if he'd swollen to twice his normal size.

Ripper panted beside him. The dog lifted his head and Penny stiffened as he seemed to stare straight at her, but then he bent to pick up something small and limp from the ground.

'Wishyouwas!' The word burst from Penny's mouth before she could stop it.

Scrawl's head snapped up and he swivelled round, still in a crouch. 'You!' he snarled. 'Meddling, ungrateful maggot! I should have put *you* in the shredder!'

'You killed him!' she cried.

Scrawl snorted. 'What use would a dead one be to me?' He plucked Wishyouwas from Ripper's jaws and shook him. 'It's the shock makes them go like this. Quite a handy little helper he'll be, once I've trained him to do what he's told.'

'You can't!' she said.

Scrawl's mouth curled upwards. 'I can. And if you tell anyone where I've gone, it'll be worse for your little friend.'

So fast Penny almost missed it, Wishyouwas opened one eye and winked, then fell back like a limp rag.

Penny hoped the smog hid her face as a shred of hope made her heart quicken. She glanced around for something to defend him with, but could only see dropped envelopes. Then she felt in her coat pocket and her fingers closed on a thin, twisted piece of metal. Her mind raced.

'No,' Penny said. 'I mean it won't work – he won't be able to steal without this. Sorters need a special tool to find letters.' She held up the lock picker. 'See?'

Scrawl's eyes narrowed. 'Give it to me,' he said, crooking his fingers.

Penny stepped back. 'No.'

Scrawl heaved himself up with a rustle, weighed down by his overstuffed coat. Several envelopes plopped out of his pockets. '*Now*,' he snarled, twisting his hand into a claw. He stepped closer. Penny backed off, leading him further away from the hole.

'Give it to me!' Scrawl lost patience and lunged forwards. In the same instant Wishyouwas sprang to life, curled around his wrist and bit him on the finger, hard.

Scrawl yelled and flung his arm up. Wishyouwas flew through the air like a furry tennis ball and almost missed Penny's shoulder, just clinging to her collar by his fingertips. She held him and swung round to run, but a hand grabbed her collar and yanked her backwards. She shrieked and fell in the snow, all the breath knocked out of her.

Wishyouwas tumbled out of her arms and was instantly snatched up by Ripper. Penny gulped as Scrawl dragged her backwards, half throttling her.

'I gave you a chance!' he spat, hauling her to the edge of the manhole. She tried to twist and writhe away, but Scrawl put a boot on her back, forcing her to peer down into the stinking, freezing darkness.

The rush and hiss of icy water crashed against her ears. Half-frozen slime oozed over the top rung of a ladder a few feet down.

'There's ways to get out again if you know where to go,' Scrawl said, leaning down. An envelope fluttered out of his pocket past Penny's head. It floated down, down, down – before being snatched away, a tiny white rectangle on a black, fast-flowing river. 'As long as you don't fall into the water, that is.' Scrawl chuckled. He dragged her further forwards until her top half was tipping over the edge and she had to cling to the sides to stop herself plunging in. 'Any last words?'

Penny felt a sob swell in her chest. She ignored Scrawl and looked up instead. The smog parted for a moment. In the patch of night sky she saw the small, blinking lights of a plane, flying high above London. *Mum*, she thought, as time seemed to slow down.

Then she saw something else.

At first she thought she'd imagined it ... but no! A small, winged object shot across the patch of darkness. And then another!

'What's that?' Scrawl hissed, peering upwards. Penny strained her neck round, in time to see a triangular hang-glider plummet out of the smog and bounce off his head.

'Argh!' Scrawl screeched as another dived at him out of nowhere. Penny saw the flicker of paws and tail, and her heart surged.

Ripper whined and backed off, his jaws still clamped around Wishyouwas.

'Get away!' Scrawl released Penny. She gasped, almost falling into the manhole, but managed to steady herself and wriggled backwards as fast as she could. Stolen envelopes spilt out of Scrawl's over-stuffed coat and rained around her as he punched his arms wildly in the air.

Penny heard the papery crunch of the gliders crash-landing on the snow. By the time she wobbled to her feet, no more flew from the sky. Scrawl's eyes were bloodshot and scratches criss-crossed his face. He grabbed Penny before she could run and pressed his long fingernail into her neck, shooting a needle-like pain through her skin.

'It'll take more than a bunch of flying rats to stop me!' he said.

'Let Dear Penny go,' growled a gruff voice. From behind a crumpled hang-glider, a squat, six-inch-high shape emerged through the smog.

Then another the same size as the first appeared. Fragile and Handlewithcare muscled their way closer to Scrawl aiming sharpened pencils, their fur darker than Penny had ever seen.

'Ha!' The rat catcher's nose wrinkled. 'Think I'm scared of *you*? Ripper – hunt!'

But the greyhound whined, still holding on to Wishyouwas, and looked at his master.

'Useless mutt! I want you to get *all* of them, not just one!' Scrawl aimed a vicious kick at his dog.

Ripper yelped and tossed his head. Penny heard a sound like ripping paper and a squeal of agony as Wishyouwas was flung through the air, landing somewhere out of sight with a dull thud.

'Wishyouwas!' she screamed, struggling, but Scrawl's nail dug in deeper.

Ripper lowered his head and stalked towards the guards, about to attack.

'I think not!' cried a familiar voice from above. Penny gasped and looked up as one final hang-glider swooped into sight. She glimpsed Thiswayup strapped to Posthaste. The old Solver brandished his crutch as they rose on a gust of wind. 'Fancy another leg, do you?' he cried. 'Well, not today!' The glider dipped towards Ripper and the sharp point of Thiswayup's compass glinted as it landed deep in the dog's bottom.

Ripper leaped in the air. Tucking his tail between his legs, the dog rocketed out of sight. Thiswayup let out a hoot of triumph as the hang-glider landed in the snow.

'*You!*' Scrawl's eyes bulged. He let go of Penny to charge at Thiswayup. An aerial assault of pencils from the guards flew at his head. Scrawl staggered, throwing his hands in front of his face.

Penny ran towards where Wishyouwas had fallen. She found him curled against the alley wall, lying stiff and still in the snow. She gathered his small, cold body into her arms. Most of his tail was torn clean off, in the same place the trap had wounded him. She pulled out her uncle's handker-chief to staunch the bleeding.

Meanwhile Scrawl stomped and stamped, trying to squash the Sorters beneath his boots. As he did so a waterfall of envelopes tumbled out of his over-coat. He looked as if he were shrinking.

'My valuables!' He bent down, trying to scoop them up, but the guards only harassed him even more, jabbing him in the hands.

Scrawl's breath came out in ragged gasps. 'I surrender!' he said suddenly, arms up. 'You win!'

The Sorters backed down, eyeing him warily.

'I never meant to hurt you,' Scrawl said, his voice soft and wheedling. 'I only wanted my fair share, honest!' At the same time he took a step back towards the open manhole, his eyes darting like a rat's.

'Let me go,' he said, taking another backwards step. 'Don't tell anyone it was me and I'll never steal another letter again, on my life!'

'Prove it,' growled Fragile, hopping closer.

Scrawl put his hands in his pockets and pulled

out the last of his envelopes. He held them up, hesitated, then sneered and spun towards the manhole.

But his boot skidded on a dropped envelope. Scrawl lost his balance, waving his arms like propellers. His mouth opened as he fell forwards and stepped into thin air, before plunging down the hole. His screech of terror was followed by a far-down, distant splash.

The Sorters peered over the edge of the hole.

'Bon voyage,' Handlewithcare muttered.

'Dear Penny! Are you hurt?' Thiswayup hobbled up to her and put a paw on her knee.

Penny shook her head, unable to speak. Her tears dripped on to Wishyouwas's damp, blood-stained fur. She'd wrapped his wounded tail but still couldn't feel any movement at all. He lay motion-less in her hands, as small and balled up as when she'd first found him in the drawer at the post office.

Thiswayup's face drooped like a melted candle. Postehaste, Fragile and Handlewithcare appeared around her, their chins sunk low.

They suddenly moved away, merging into the smog as Penny heard uneven footsteps.

'Can I see?' asked a familiar voice.

Penny blinked and looked up into Uncle Frank's bristly face.

'I would've got here quicker if ma stick hadn't broken,' he said, grunting as he knelt beside her. 'Not to mention seeing ma way through the smog!'

'It's all my fault,' Penny said with a choke.

'You know, after ma beloved dog Penfold was killed by a bomb blast, I thought I'd lost the ability to care about anyone,' her uncle said, at the same time gently taking Wishyouwas from her. 'It hurt too much. But the thing *you've* since taught me –' he held the small body against his ear – 'is nothing you love is ever truly lost.' He started rubbing Wishyouwas's fur with his uniform sleeve. 'Come on, wee fellow,' he muttered.

Penny leaned close, desperate for any sign, but there was no movement at all, his paws limp and lifeless. Penny held one to her cheek.

She jumped as Wishyouwas's fingers twitched. Then all of a sudden his chest rose and fell with a soft sigh.

'He's alive!' Penny cried and laughed at the same time.

Uncle Frank seemed to have something in his eye. He wiped it away, then passed Wishyouwas back to her and wrapped an arm around her shoulders. 'Don't worry, Pen,' he said, giving her a squeeze. 'He'll soon be back on his feet … I mean, paws.'

22

All Sorted

Wishyouwas awoke in Penny's arms with a shudder. But as his moonlike eyes opened, his cheeks lifted in a smile.

'D-Dear P-Penny!' he stuttered, still coming round. He frowned. 'I s-sound like Withlove.'

'No, you don't!' snapped Withlove. The little Gatherer was the other patient in the temporary sick bay that had been set up in the Postmaster General's office. She lay curled up on the desk, inside his in tray, with a fresh handkerchief spread over her as a blanket.

Penny could have sworn Wishyouwas blushed. She laughed and gave him a squeeze, then grimaced. 'I'm sorry! Your poor tail …'

Wishyouwas squirmed round and peered at his behind. Only three inches remained of his tail, bandaged in gauze. His ears drooped, but only for a moment. 'I doesn't need all of it anyway,' he said. Then his head tilted towards the doorway. Muffled talking and laughing came from behind it. Wishyouwas gave Penny a wondering look.

'Come and see!' she said, swivelling round in the Postmaster General's chair. She sprang up and opened the door, which led on to a vast sorting room. Wishyouwas held on to her thumb and his small mouth fell open.

A huge mound of mail had been retrieved from the underground workshop. The Sorters worked at long tables alongside the Royal Mail staff, replacing stolen postal orders, cheques and banknotes inside letters and cards so fast their paws were a blur. Penny even spotted Their Highnesses inspecting letters through a pair of spectacles. Stampduty was positioned on a high stack of books with the mega-phone in front of him, reading rapidly from the scraps of notepaper he had brought from the work-shop. Thanks to him, they knew exactly what had to be re-sorted where.

Wishyouwas's voice was full of awe. 'We has never sorted *with* humans before.'

Postal workers ran backwards and forwards, hauling full sacks from the tables towards a wide entrance that led on to the street, where a row of Royal Mail vans waited to deliver the cards and parcels.

Penny spotted Thiswayup waving to them from a nearby table and carried Wishyouwas over.

'Ah, my boy!' the Solver said above the urgent rustling of paper. 'I *am* glad to see you finally awake. Shame about the tail, but it is surprising how much ingenuity it brings when you must make do and mend.'

Uncle Frank hobbled over to them on a borrowed walking stick, smiling. 'The Postmaster General said we'll deliver everything just in time for

Christmas, thanks to the Sorters offering to help,' he said. 'It would have been a national disaster otherwise!'

There was a sudden commotion near the post room entrance. Sorters leaped on to ceiling lights with frightened squeaks. Penny looked round and spotted a streak of fur weaving between the worktables and chairs, trailing a length of rope.

'It's Ripper!' she cried.

'Hold this.' Uncle Frank gave Penny his stick. He hobbled a few paces, put his fingers in his mouth and whistled.

The greyhound snapped its head in Uncle Frank's direction. Penny held Wishyouwas close as the dog bounded towards them, tongue lolling.

'*Sit!*' Uncle Frank boomed.

Ripper skidded to a halt, scrabbling on the lino floor. The dog dropped to its haunches, panting hard.

Uncle Frank slowly raised his hand. Then, darting his hand out, he ruffled the greyhound's sleek head. Ripper let out a strange noise like a cough and then, unexpectedly, woofed.

'There you are, boy,' Uncle Frank said, tickling the greyhound's ears. 'You're safe now.'

'He can't stay here. What about the Sorters?' Penny said. 'He tried to kill them!'

'Oh, I think perhaps his postage has been paid,' remarked Thiswayup. 'And after this experience, I doubt he will be much of a threat to us.'

'He only did what Scrawl forced him to do,' agreed Uncle Frank. 'There's good in every creature.' He led the greyhound by his lead inside the Postmaster General's office. Penny followed, still unsure.

Withlove hopped out of her bed as Ripper came in, bent over the Postmaster General's desk and squeaked, 'Boo!'

Ripper yelped and leaped behind Uncle Frank's legs.

'See?' he said, laughing. He bent down and looked into the greyhound's eyes. 'Hermes,' he said. 'A new name for a new life. Come and live with me, eh, boy? I can offer a good wage in biscuits. Anyway, I'll need some company once Penny's gone home.'

'Oh …' Penny said, feeling an unexpected sadness sweep over her. She'd enjoyed getting to know Uncle Frank, and once she went home she wouldn't have the chance to see Wishyouwas, if he ever came gathering again. He curled his paw around her finger, seeming to feel the same way.

Together they watched from the office doorway as the workers shouldered sack after sack out of the post room. Dawn was breaking as the line of Royal Mail vans dwindled, until there was only one left.

'That's it!' a postwoman stood up and cried. 'The last letter's sorted!'

A huge cheer went up. Everyone in the post room was on their paws and feet, clapping.

'Hip-hip for Penny and the Sorters!' bellowed the Postmaster General. The hoorays were shouted back with gusto, and Penny felt her whole face turn red, while Wishyouwas swelled into a ball.

But as the last van sped away, in its place a black car appeared with a blue light on top. A group of

police officers climbed out, staring in astonishment at the scene before them. The Postmaster General marched over and took them to one side. Penny couldn't hear what he was saying, but his voice grew louder and angrier. Then one of the officers pointed straight at Penny and shook his head.

She glanced at her uncle, who'd seen them too. 'Let me find oot what's happening,' he said, leading Hermes with him. After a minute he returned, his face pale. 'They found Scrawl,' he said. 'He was clinging to a sewer ladder like a drooned rat. He'll be going to prison for a long time. But –' he swallowed – 'the police want us to come with them. The Sorters too.'

'But the Sorters haven't done anything wrong!' Penny protested. 'Scrawl *made* them open the letters!'

'I tried telling them that,' he said. 'The Postmaster General explained too. But their orders come from the highest authority, whatever that means. I'm certain once everything's understood, they'll let us go.'

But Penny wasn't certain at all. The police officers strode towards them with stony faces. 'Come with us, please,' said one of them. 'Quickly and quietly now.'

'I will join you,' said the Postmaster General, straightening his jacket. 'The Sorters are as much under my care now as any of my human staff.'

Worry wormed a hole in Penny's stomach as she put on her coat and followed the police out of Headquarters, carrying Wishyouwas and Withlove inside her recovered satchel. She climbed into a police car beside Uncle Frank, leaving Hermes in the care of the emergency warden. Further along the pavement, she saw the exhausted Sorters clambering inside a large police van; the type without any windows.

Penny tried asking questions, but the police officer in front said nothing, so she peered out of the window as they sped through the streets. Sunlight was breaking through the clouds and the wind blew, sweeping the smog away to reveal pretty lights twinkling in windows and holly wreaths dangling from door knockers. London was being unwrapped like a glittering Christmas present, only not for them.

She felt a nudge in her ribs.

'Look, Penny!' Uncle Frank said, leaning forwards and pointing.

At the end of a long, wide road ahead of them was a plinth with a statue of an angel on top. Behind that, spread out like a wedding cake, lay a huge, gleaming white building Penny recognised from photographs. Dozens of windows glittered in the sunlight and at the top a colourful flag fluttered in the breeze.

'Where is we, Dear Penny?' Wishyouwas asked, as the police car drew up to a set of tall black gates. Guards with red coats and bearskin hats saluted them as they drove through and slowed to a halt.

'I – I think ...' she stammered, hardly able to believe it, until a smartly dressed butler opened the car door and bowed.

'Welcome,' he said, 'to Buckingham Palace.'

23

The Royal Postmistress

'Please follow me,' said the butler, ushering them out of the car and through a door in the side of the palace. Bewildered, Penny followed his skimming steps along a carpeted corridor and through another door. As it opened her breath caught. They stood inside an enormous hall, flanked by shining suits of armour. Two golden staircases spiralled up to meet at a central balcony above their heads.

The Postmaster General came in behind them and stood almost as straight as the armour. Uncle

Frank licked his hand and frantically tried to flatten his hair.

Penny heard a soft pattering and looked round to see Sorters gathering in a large huddle behind her, their eyes bulging. Penny lowered Wishyouwas and Withlove to the gleaming marble floor. 'This is where the Royal Postmistress lives!' she whispered to them.

Wishyouwas clutched her finger. 'Does you think she finded out about the stamp you gived me, Dear Penny?'

Penny laughed. 'I don't think she'll mind that.'

'Please wait here,' said the butler, once they were all gathered. 'Her Majesty will be with you in a moment.'

Almost at once a door opened at the top of the stairs, and Penny's tummy flipped over. A pretty young woman in a blue satin dress stepped on to the balcony. Her face was instantly familiar, her brown hair curled into soft waves beneath a diamond tiara. She smiled down at them, and with a collective thump the Sorters fell flat on their stomachs, until the Queen, reaching the bottom of the stairs, waved her hand for them to rise.

'Good morning,' she said with a smile. 'I have invited you all here to share Christmas Eve with me and my family, as a small token of gratitude for the very great service you have given our country.'

The Queen swept towards a set of double doors. They were opened instantly by two footmen, revealing a magnificent dining room so huge that Penny thought Uncle Frank's entire post office could have fitted inside it. Crystal chandeliers sparkled beneath a ceiling painted with cherubs. In one corner a Christmas tree taller than a double-decker bus blazed with real candles. A long, gleaming wooden table took up most of the room, decked out with pure white linen and ornate silver cutlery, surrounded by golden chairs. But best of all, the entire table was covered from end to end with silver platters piled high with food. There were cakes frosted with snow-like icing sugar, fancy French pastries, jewel-coloured jellies and jams, mince pies, crackers with every type of cheese, roasted chestnuts, sandwiches with dozens of different fillings … everything you could ever dream of eating. The centrepiece of the banquet was a magnificent three-tiered Christmas cake covered with glossy royal icing. Penny felt her eyes widen. There were even custard creams!

'Now I *know* I am dreaming,' Thiswayup murmured, clasping his paws. 'Such scenes only exist on Christmas cards.'

The Queen heard him. 'Please sit,' she said, gesturing to the table. 'I assure you it is all quite real.'

The Sorters clambered and hopped on to the chairs, which were stacked high with cushions. They stared longingly at the delicious food but were too polite to take any. Penny sat silently beside Uncle Frank. Nobody seemed to know what to say or do.

Then the doors burst open and two little children ran in and shrieked with delight. Behind them marched the Queen's husband, accompanied by the butler.

'Children! What did I tell you? You must *not* get overexcited,' the Queen scolded them. 'I must apologise.' She blushed.

After that everyone relaxed and the air filled with happy chatter. The Sorters fell on the food. The Postmaster General spoke with the Queen, who sat at the head of the table. Penny grinned as she saw Thiswayup deep in conversation with her husband – something to do with aeroplanes – while cramming his mouth with biscuits between sentences. The tiny Sorters from the school clambered up and slid down the velvet curtains, chased by the little Prince and Princess.

While tea, coffee and thimbles of fruit juice were being served, Penny took a deep breath and edged up to the Queen.

'I – I wondered if I could ask you something, Your Majesty?' she stammered.

'You just have,' answered the Queen.

'Oh, no, I mean—'

'My little joke,' the Queen replied, her eyes twinkling. 'What may I do for you?'

Penny looked down the table to where Wishyouwas was sharing a jam tart with Withlove. She didn't want him to find out what she was going to ask, so she whispered her question to the Queen. If the amount of jam on Wishyouwas's nose was anything to go by, he hadn't overheard.

The Queen folded her napkin and nodded. 'I shall see to it at once,' she said, rising. Penny hurried back to her seat. The room hushed.

'I should like to say a few words,' said the Queen. 'First of all, the Postmaster General has informed me that until now, the Royal Mail has been unaware of the Sorters' existence.' She raised her eyebrows at

Dearsir and Dearmadam, the same look Uncle Frank gave Penny when he caught her writing a letter on the window sill.

'Y-Your Royal Postmistress,' Dearsir stammered. 'We felt it wise to keep our lives a secret from humans.'

'I understand your need for caution,' replied the Queen. 'You met with too much distrust, for far too long, which forced you to live your lives in secret. But considering that you provide such an important service for the *Royal* Mail, I hope you will allow

myself and everyone who works there to treat you as our equals?'

Dearsir and Dearmadam nodded. 'We will, Your Royal Postmistress!'

'Very good,' said the Queen. 'I therefore declare the Lost Letter Bureau formally open! The Royal Mail with provide you with everything you need to perform your duties, beginning with the humane removal of the rats. The Bureau and your existence will remain top secret. Is that not correct, Postmaster General?'

He stood and nodded. 'All Royal Mail staff have already sworn an oath of secrecy,' he said. 'After everything the Sorters have done for us today and in the past, they were glad to do so, Your Majesty.'

An excited chattering swept round the table, and Wishyouwas smiled at Penny. Finally the Sorters would be safe!

The Queen raised her hand for quiet. 'Will Penelope Black please come forward?'

Penny stumbled off her chair and walked to the head of the table. She stood before the Queen, who fastened a medal to her dress. It was an eight-pointed silver star. The words around the edge read: *For Faithful Service.*

The room burst into cheers and applause. Only Uncle Frank didn't clap, as his hands were busy mopping his eyes with a handkerchief.

The Queen raised her hand once more. 'I understand that you have a system of ranks and classes,' she said, facing the Sorters. 'I respect this and have no wish to interfere in your way of life. Yet I do hope that, when an exceptional case arises, you will consider my recommendation?'

Their Highnesses bowed their heads in agreement. 'We will, Your Royal Postmistress,' they said in unison.

'Thank you,' said the Queen. 'Would the Gatherer known as Wishyouwas please come forward?'

Wishyouwas seemed frozen solid. He stared blankly ahead of him, until Withlove gave him a gentle shove. Wobbling a little, he hopped off the chair and shuffled up beside Penny. He bowed until his nose touched the carpet.

The Queen nodded to her butler, who brought forwards a tray upon which rested a silver letter knife. 'Wishyouwas, you have sacrificed more than any other Sorter today in performing your duty,' she said. 'At Christmas it is customary to bestow honours on those who have shown exemplary service, courage or skill. You have shown all three.' She signalled to Penny, who lifted Wishyouwas up in trembling hands.

The Queen lightly touched Wishyouwas on his head and shoulders with the letter knife. 'I hereby upgrade Wishyouwas to the rank of ... Deliverer, First Class.'

The room exploded with squeaks and cheers.

'Bravo!' cried Thiswayup.

Wishyouwas gazed at Penny, his eyes sparkling like two diamonds.

24

The Last Letter

Penny awoke at the post office on Christmas morning and blinked hard. The events of yesterday seemed like a dream. A feast with the Queen, Wishyouwas upgraded, and the Sorters safe at last! She felt under her pillow and pulled out her silver medal, running her thumb over the words around the edge.

She heard 'Silent Night' floating up from the kitchen wireless and a thread of sadness wove itself through the happy memories of the day before. Now Wishyouwas was a Deliverer, he wouldn't gather letters from the post office any more. She didn't know when she'd see him again, just like she didn't know when Mum would come back.

She shook herself and tried to buck up. At least she still had Uncle Frank to spend Christmas with. She dressed, opened the door and went down the stairs. Over the carol, she heard a woman's voice humming along. And it wasn't coming from the wireless …

'Mum!' she shouted, leaping the last three steps and bursting into the kitchen.

Her mother sat at the table in her sky-blue pilot's uniform, her ginger hair ruffled as if she hadn't slept. As Penny flew in, she leaped up almost as fast as a Sorter and swept her off her feet. 'Penny, ma wee girl! I've missed you so much!' she said, whirling her round. 'I'm sorry I've been away so long. I flew back to Glasgow two nights ago – it was so hard to pass right over London on the way and know I couldn't land, and you so close! There were no passenger trains to London at *all* yesterday, so I cadged a lift with the Night Mail and arrived an hour ago!' She put Penny down and raised an eyebrow. 'And it seems you've had your fair share of adventure too! Frank's been telling me everything. I could hardly believe it until …' She smiled. 'Well, anyway.' She fished a handful of envelopes out of her pocket. 'I wrote you a letter every day,' she said. 'An airmail pilot with no way to send a letter. Can you believe it!'

Uncle Frank cleared his throat. He was standing at the stove, with Hermes peacefully asleep in a sack-lined parcel box beside him. '*Talking* of letters,' he said, dipping a wooden spoon inside the kettle to fish out an egg, 'there's a wee bit of sorting I need you to do in the post office, Penny, before breakfast.'

Penny's face dropped. 'But there's no post on Christmas Day,' she said. 'And Mum's only just got back ...'

Her mother steered her out of the kitchen. 'Come back when you're done. I'll still be here!' she said, smiling as she shut the kitchen door behind her. Penny frowned and traipsed through the hallway. Why were they both acting so strangely all of a sudden?

She opened the post office door, stepped inside and gasped.

The curtains were drawn, yet bright lights dazzled her eyes. Candles and tealights covered the counter. Streamers made from coloured paper festooned the ceiling, and a small Christmas tree stood in a bucket in the middle of the floor, frosted with *real* snow. But how ... ?

'Merry Christmas, Dear Penny!' squeaked a voice. Wishyouwas appeared at the top of the tree. Around his neck glinted a medallion made from the dial of a wristwatch, the symbol of the Deliverers.

With a wobbly leap he sprang on to the floor and ran up to her, then clambered on to her shoulder, a little slower than usual. But his fur was just as warm, and it tickled her cheek as he wrapped his paws around her neck.

Penny tingled with happiness. 'You're here!' she said.

She heard a noise on the shelves behind her. From behind pen pots, piles of pamphlets and boxes of paperclips emerged Felicitations, Withlove, Fragile and Handlewithcare. Lastly, Thiswayup hobbled out from behind the till, a little plumper from all the custard creams he'd enjoyed the previous day.

'Glad tidings to you, Dear Penny!' he said, tapping forwards on his crutch. 'I hope you do not mind the interruption. Their Highnesses would have been here themselves, but they and Stampduty are overseeing urgent repairs to The Bureau.' He raised a paw to his mouth and added in a hushed voice, his misty eyes twinkling, 'I would sell my stamps to watch the Postmaster General's face when he sees Stampduty's list! However, we had a *most* important delivery to make. Wishyouwas, would you … ?'

Wishyouwas hopped on to the counter and wriggled inside the lost letter drawer, which was already ajar. He reappeared holding a small parcel wrapped in brown paper. 'We maked you this, Dear Penny,' he said, holding it out a little shyly.

The Sorters shuffled round to watch as Penny untied the string and unwrapped a small box. She opened the lid to find a nest of shredded letter paper, on which rested a strange circular object. It was a watch dial like Wishyouwas's, only instead of hour and minute hands, a paperclip ticked to mark the time. It was framed inside a silver-rimmed monocle, attached to a thin chain looped round to make a necklace. As Penny turned it over in her hand, the glass caught the light and glittered, like a Sorter's eye.

Felicitations laid her paw on Penny's hand. 'It represents all of us,' she said. 'The lock picker is the symbol of the Gatherers, the clock is the symbol of the Deliverers, who must *always* be on time –' she raised an eyebrow at Wishyouwas, who shuffled on his paws – 'and the monocle is the symbol of the Solvers. With this, you will forever be welcome to visit us at The Bureau, Dear Penny.'

Fragile and Handlewithcare nodded. 'Lifetime entry pass,' they said together.

'It's beautiful,' Penny said. 'I wish I had something for you too.'

'You have already given us more than we could ever have imagined,' answered Thiswayup. 'We would have been lost without you. Not to mention the Christmas post.'

His words jogged Penny's memory. 'Wait! There's one more letter!' She turned to Wishyouwas. 'When we first climbed into the postbox, remember? It fell on my head and I put it in my satchel ...'

'I already g-gathered it, Dear Penny!' squeaked Withlove with a shy smile.

'And I have already solved it,' Thiswayup admitted. 'It passed the time admirably well, while the others were decorating.' He hobbled back behind the till and pulled out a white envelope with the tip of his compass, which he laid on the counter in front of Penny.

After its long adventure, the address on the envelope was smudged and hard to decipher, but, peering closely, Penny could read Thiswayup's tiny, neat handwriting at the top: *Mr Andrews, 22 Hornsey Lane, London.*

Penny looked up with a start. 'That's the old gentleman customer!' she said.

Thiswayup tapped the envelope. 'From the thickness of the paper and from holding it to the light, I would bet my best stamps it is an invitation,' he said.

Penny felt a tingle run through her. Perhaps Mr Andrews wouldn't be spending Christmas alone after all!

'The address isn't far, Dear Penny,' said Wishyouwas, hopping forwards to pick up the envelope. Suddenly his ears drooped and he fiddled with the medallion around his neck. 'Does ... you want to come?' he asked her.

Penny pulled her own medallion over her head. 'Try and stop me!' she said with a grin.

Wishyouwas clambered on to her shoulder, clutching her plait in one paw and the envelope in the other. As she opened the post office door, he whispered in her ear, 'I is forever your friend, Dear Penny.'

Penny felt warm all the way to her toes. She smiled at him, and his eyes sparkled in the sunlight. 'And I'm forever yours,' she said.

Post Office Underground Railway ——
Abandoned Lines - - - - -

Islington

ROSS STATION

Hornsey
Lane
P.O.

Scribe's
End

HACKNEY

NT PLEASANT POST OFFICE
AL MAIL HEADQUARTERS

N

W   E

S

King Edward Building
Post Office

LIVERPOOL
STREET STATION

WHITECHAPEL

Eastern District
Post Office

Western Central
District Post Office

T
H
A
M
E
S

WATERLOO
STATION

Lambeth

Vauxhall

Author's Note

Wishyouwas sprang into my life while I was walking to work one chilly winter's day. I was passing by a building near where the first Penny Post was founded. I began to imagine a story about a girl getting lost in the post, and moments later Wishyouwas's name popped into my head. Penny and the determined little Gatherer demanded to be written about. Luckily when I was seven, I had visited the Mail Rail – or the Post Office Railway as it used to be called. Not many people knew then about the secret railway running beneath their feet, shuttling letters and parcels between Paddington and Whitechapel. And even fewer know the reason why whenever a letter is lost, it always eventually turns up where it rightfully belongs ...

Acknowledgements

Dearest Reader

Many Sorters feature in this story, but there are others who don't appear on these pages. I would like to mention them briefly, as each and every one has played an important role in bringing this book to life.

Firstly I give my eternal gratitude to the Gatherers in my world:

To my husband, best friend and writing companion, Andy, for Sorter-seeking around the world with me, reading and editing more drafts than I dare count, and being by my side for every step of this extraordinary journey. To my daughter Isabella – I made up my mind to finish writing this story in time for you to read it, and this achievement is only pipped by making you. To my dad, Julian, for reading to me every night growing up and instilling the soul of a storyteller in me, and to my stepmum, Lolly, who took me exploring through London and once left a note that helped sow the seed for Wishyouwas. To my mum, Catherine, and stepdad, Adam, for unwaveringly encouraging my writing since the very beginning. To my sister Tiff, whose own words burned a path towards possibility long before I set out, and my sister Anna, without whom this book may still not be in existence – thank you for helping me find my way when I was truly lost. To my brother, Chris, for giving me the courage to make a difficult call. To Sandra and Ian Hardy, and my mother-in-law Barbara Blount, for their excellent proofreading and endless belief. To my lovely friends Maddy, Lou, Sara, Marcelle, Pete and Yvonne for always being there and wishing me luck. And to my wonderful critique group, who have shared my writing highs and lows throughout the years – Cristina Boyton, Liz Heron, Liz Kashyap, Lauren Evans, Emma Gladding, Tracy Curran and Emily Ann Davison. I would especially like to reach out a paw to Ivan, my first child reader, who gave me some very wise advice.

Next to the wonderful Solvers, who helped turn my scribbles into a story:

I owe a parcel-load of thanks to Christabel McKinley, my amazing agent and Wishyouwas-equivalent, for taking a leap of faith in me and my stories. We stumbled across each other and I will forever be glad we did. To Allison Cole, Livvy Hickman, Camille Burns and Penelope Killick at David Higham Associates, for putting so much heart into sending this story out into the world. To Stuart White, the writing world's answer to Thiswayup, for his incredible mentorship, friendship and fellowship. To all the 2019 WriteMentor Children's Novel Award and

Times/Chicken House readers and judges who voted for *Wishyouwas* and gave me so much faith to carry on. I would also like to thank Kathryn Price and Helen Corner-Bryant at Cornerstones for their early editorial advice and encouragement.

I must mention the wonderful staff at the Postal Museum in London, who have inspired, helped and encouraged this story to be told through their own Sorter-like discoveries, hard work and dedication.

And finally to the Deliverers, who ventured many extra miles to bring this book home:

Thank you to everyone in the Bloomsbury family who believed in *Wishyouwas* with such passion it literally left me speechless: Hannah Sandford, my brilliant editor-in-chief and all-round *Wishyouwas* fanatic; Fliss Stevens, Nick de Somogyi and Anna Swan for making sure no errors sneaked into the copy; Sarah Baldwin for your incredible design; Beatrice Cross and Kat McKenna for your Publicity and Marketing might; Sally Wilks, Laura Main Ellen, Sonia Palmisano and all the Sales team for giving *Wishyouwas* so much of your time and attention; and to the Bloomsbury Production team – I salute you.

Of course, the Sorters' story was only words before it was brought to life by my story-partner, Penny Neville-Lee, who has transformed it into something truly magical. Thank you for every pencil stroke.

But my biggest thanks goes to you, Dear Reader, for holding this book in your hands. You are the reason for it being here at all. I hope you enjoyed joining Wishyouwas and Penny on this adventure, and I sincerely hope that you'll return for the next chapter.

Forever yours
Alexandra x

There's more excitement in the post!

WISHYOUWAS

WILL RETURN
IN A BRAND-NEW ADVENTURE

When Wishyouwas and Penny are entrusted
with a top-secret mission by the Royal
Postmistress herself, they uncover a deadly
plot to derail her coronation … Can they
stop the traitors in their tracks?

Coming soon!

About the Author

Alexandra Page spent her early childhood being airmailed between England and Zimbabwe and making up stories to entertain her younger sisters and brother. After studying English Literature at University College London, she worked for several years in book production and then in the City, before venturing into writing. This is Alexandra's first children's book. *Wishyouwas* won the WriteMentor Children's Novel Award in 2019 and was also shortlisted for the Times/Chicken House Children's Fiction Competition. Alexandra loves being creative, travelling to far-flung places and swimming in anything bigger than a puddle. She lives in London with her husband and daughter.

About the Illustrator

Penny Neville-Lee was raised on a healthy diet of Saturday cartoons and MGM musicals. Never happier than when creating, she spent her early years drawing and making, and was rarely found without a doodle somewhere in the margins. Penny studied for a Painting MA at the Royal College of Art. After several years making large oil paintings of gloomy woods in the company of Radio 4 and some studio mice, she had her small son, shifted to the kitchen table and realised there might be something in those doodles after all. Penny is inspired by small people, bright colours, a blank page and newly sharpened pencils. She lives in Manchester with her two children, husband and very adventurous cat.